Jake's Bride

Jake's Bride

Search for Love Series

KAREN ROSE SMITH

ABOUT THE AUTHOR

Karen Rose Smith

Award-winning author Karen Rose Smith was born in Pennsylvania. Although she was an only child, she remembers the bonds of an extended family. Since her father came from a family of ten and her mother, a family of seven, there were always aunts, uncles and cousins visiting on weekends. Family is a strong theme in her books and she suspects her childhood memories are the reason.

In college, Karen began writing poetry and also met her husband-to-be. They both began married life as teachers, but when their son was born, Karen decided to try her hand at a home-decorating business. She returned to teaching for a while but changes in her life led her to writing romance fiction. Now she writes romances and mysteries full time. She has sold over 80 novels since 1991.

Presently, she is hard at work on a series for Harlequin Special Edition as well as the Caprice De Luca home stager mystery series for Kensington Books. When she isn't writing, she cares for three rescue cats, gardens, and cooks.

Married to her college sweetheart since 1971, believing in the power of love and commitment, she envisions herself writing relationship novels, both romance and mystery, for a long time to come!

For more about Karen and her latest releases, visit her websites at www.karenrosesmith.com and www.karenrose smithmysteries.com. To keep in touch day to day, follow Karen on Facebook at KarenRoseSmithBooks, on Twitter @ karenrosesmith, on her Cats, Roses...and Books! blog and her IN TOUCH with Karen Rose Smith e-zine.

Jake's Bride

Prologue

Sara Standish's heart thudded with excitement, but with trepidation, too, as she climbed the porch steps to the house where she'd lived all her twenty years. Surely, Jake would change his mind about not having children once he heard her news. With their wedding two days away and their future stretching before them, wouldn't he feel joy over a life they'd created together?

But then she remembered the pain in his voice, on his face, in his hands, the night he'd told her about his wife and child...how he'd lost them...how he never wanted to experience that devastation again. Her empathy had turned into kisses that turned into making love for the first time. He'd needed her and she'd needed him. But afterward, he'd vowed he wouldn't make love to her again until their wedding night, until she was protected, until they were truly husband and wife. He was that type of man.

Although she loved children, she'd agreed to a childless marriage. She loved Jake so much she'd agree to almost anything.

Did he love her enough to let go of his past and accept this child?

Sara knew she'd agreed to a childless marriage, praying that some day, knowing the love Jake had to give, he would change his mind. She'd witnessed his work at the community center with teenagers who could stray from an honest path too easily. And he didn't express his feelings often, but he did love her. He'd showed her that with the yellow roses he brought her every Friday night. Each rose signified the completion of another week, their growing feelings for each other, the importance of talking about their successes and failures. Those special times of holding and caring were more precious to her than she could ever explain. The two most recent roses in a vase on her desk in her bedroom reminded her daily of the commitment they'd made.

She loved Jake so. Still, her fear made her throat tight. What if he couldn't accept this child? What if...

Stopping the questions, she opened the door and went inside. She heard voices coming from the kitchen. Her mother's and Jake's. Quickly she shrugged out of her jacket and hung it in the foyer closet. Nervously brushing her short, auburn hair away from her face, she wondered how she could get Jake alone without making her mother too curious. Maybe she could say she wanted to show him the beautiful November sunset. Or maybe she should wait to tell him after supper. They could drive to the beach...

"You're a gem, Mrs. Standish. Your pot roast could win a medal." Jake's tone was teasing but conveyed his appreciation of her mother's culinary skill.

Jennie Standish laughed. "You can tell from the aroma? I think maybe you just haven't eaten properly all day. And, by the way, Jake, don't you think since you're marrying my daughter this weekend, you could call me Jennie?"

There was a pause. "I'd like that."

Sara understood the huskiness in Jake's voice. He'd lost his own mother and appreciated the bond he was building with hers.

"Jake, there is something I'd like to discuss with you before Sara arrives."

"Is there a problem?"

Jennie Standish's tone was gentle. "I don't know. Sara tells me you don't want to have children."

He didn't answer immediately, but finally said, "That's right."

"You know Sara loves children. For three years she's worked in that day care center. I told her somehow I'd manage to send her to college full time instead of part time, but over and over she's reminded me the experience would make her a better teacher when she does get her degree. She loves working with little children. I think she'd do it even if she didn't get paid."

The house was quiet for a few moments as Sara waited for Jake's response.

"We believe our love is enough."

"Your love needs to spill over, Jake. It needs to be bigger than the two of you."

His voice was sad with a raspy catch. "You don't understand."

"Make me understand so I know Sara won't regret this pact she's made with you."

"Did Sara tell you about my wife and son?"

"She told me you're divorced."

"Yes. Because of what happened. Because—"

Sara knew Jake held in his emotions and didn't want to appear vulnerable to anyone. It came from his upbringing, from his years as a member of the police force, from the sticky situations he'd handled as a private investigator, from the loss of his son.

A chair scraped the linoleum and in her mind's eye, Sara could see Jake, his broad shoulders, his wavy black hair, his brown eyes that could hide every thought in his head so well, as he sat in the kitchen chair.

"I grew up in the projects."

"Sara did tell me that. I figured it had something to do with you becoming a police officer. But she didn't tell me why you gave it up, why you decided to become a private investigator instead."

"I became a cop because I thought I could clean up the city, make a difference. But it's not possible, Mrs. Standish." He corrected himself. "Jennie. I was a cop for eight years, and I didn't make a dent let alone a difference. You wouldn't believe the misery I saw. Then that misery touched me."

"What happened?" she asked softly.

"I was married. We had a six year old—Davie. Full of life and fun. I was working the night shift. Mary Beth and Davie decided to go for ice cream. My car was parked behind hers. Davie ran out ahead of her and opened the driver's door so he could crawl in beside her. The car exploded."

"Oh, Jake."

"I heard Mary Beth's screams. I still hear them. Neither of us could do anything. We found out later a guy I'd collared did it. It was an act of revenge. But the bomb took the wrong person, and I was to blame. Mary Beth blamed me, too. Our marriage fell apart."

"Jake, I'm so sorry."

"I won't bring a child into a world of suffering, into a world that doesn't cherish its children or protect them by keeping criminals like that thug behind bars instead of paroling them. I will never get over losing Davie. Not in this lifetime or the next. Don't you see? I can't have more children. I can't put myself through that again."

Sara leaned against the closet door. She knew his pain went deep, but she'd hoped their marriage would heal the wounds. Yet, she also knew if he wasn't ready for healing, he'd fight it. A child could make the pain deeper instead of healing him. She'd been naive to think the news of her pregnancy might be welcome. Jake said what he believed. He was passionate about what he felt. Could she trap him in a situation he didn't want? What would happen to his feelings for her?

If she told him about the baby, she knew what Jake would do. He'd go through with the wedding because he was an honorable man. But what kind of marriage would they have?

Tears flooded her eyes. Certainly a marriage he didn't want, a child who'd remind him every day of the son he'd lost. He'd resent the pain. He'd resent her. Worst of all, though he'd never admit it, he'd resent their child. She couldn't bear to see the love they'd shared erode with each passing day, each time Jake looked at her and their child and realized he was imprisoned in his anguish.

Her love wasn't strong enough to watch the feelings between them die instead of grow. Yet she had to give them one last chance, one last chance for Jake to put their love before his pain.

With trembling fingers she brushed the tears from her cheeks. Lifting her chin, she walked into the kitchen.

Jake's head came up. His brown eyes warmed just for her. Standing, he took her in his arms and hugged her. "Hi, there." His voice was still low and husky from the strain of sharing the past with her mother. "I was worried. Did you get tied up at work?"

"No. I need to talk to you. Let's go into the living room."

"But your mother has supper ready."

Jennie Standish's gaze passed quickly over the two of them, worried because she knew from the tone of Sara's voice that something was wrong. "That's all right. I can keep everything warm."

Jake took Sara's hand and walked with her to the sofa. When they were seated, he wrapped his arm around her and kissed her. Her fear kept her from responding with her usual fervor, and he leaned away, never a man to push, never a man to take more than she wanted to give.

The gold in his eyes told her better than words that his desire for her would ignite with a kiss, a touch, a smile. But she had none of them for him now. Meeting his gaze, she took a deep breath. "Jake, I need to ask you something." She unconsciously placed her hand on her stomach. "Do you think you'll ever change your mind about having children?"

The gold disappeared as his eyes darkened with pain. "Sara..."

"I want your children. And I...need to have a baby. To feel fulfilled in our marriage. To feel fulfilled as a woman." A tiny kernel of Sara inside her heart urged her to believe that her announcement might change Jake's mind, that they could have a happy future.

The nerve in his jaw worked. "We had an agreement."

A sob lodged in her throat but she pushed out the rest of what she had to say. "I know. But I can't keep it."

For a moment, she saw...devastation. And for that moment, she could see all the pain he tried to hide from the loss of his son, the depth of the wound she thought she could help heal. She'd been naive again.

Jake turned away, his lean cheeks taut. When he met her gaze again, she couldn't see anything but his dark brown eyes. He'd erected a wall...against her. She could feel it as tangibly as she'd felt his love a second before.

Stoicism marked his face as he asked, "What are you trying to tell me?"

Her heart broke and she knew it would never be the same again. She loved Jake too much to trap him. "That...that I need to have children and if you truly don't want them...then I can't marry you."

"Sara..." He spoke her name with such feeling...then all emotion was gone. "You're calling off the wedding?"

"Jake, I have to. I have to think about the future. Can't you do that? Can't you imagine—?"

He reached for her, then dropped his hand. "No, I can't. I can't imagine you pregnant, worrying day after day, night after night, whether you and the baby will be all right. I can't imagine caring for an infant, chasing after a toddler, knowing I can't protect him. And most of all, I can't imagine the aching every time I'd look at our child because I'd miss Davie even more. No, I can't imagine it, Sara, because at times even now the pain is unbearable. I can't imagine it being even worse. If you need children in your life, then you're right to call off the wedding."

He stood, moving away from her, moving out of her life. "Tell your mom I won't be staying for dinner. Tell her whatever you need to tell her."

Sara took one last chance. "Jake, you can't leave like this. We can talk—"

He shook his head. "There's nothing to talk about. We've made our choices. Now we'll have to live with them."

His tall body was rigid. She wanted to hold him and make everything right. But she couldn't. She had to let him go.

Jake Donovan didn't meet her gaze again, didn't touch her, didn't say good-bye. He simply walked out the door.

Chapter One

Almost Four Years Later

In a fog, Sara walked around the house her mother had rented in Los Angeles for most of her life. She picked up a needlework magazine on the coffee table. Crossing to her mother's favorite easy chair, she opened the tapestry bag with her mother's knitting. A small sweater was almost finished. Jennie Standish had intended it to be a Christmas present for her grandson. Christmas...a time for families and love and—

Sara had been debating with herself ever since Christopher was born—as she'd fed him, and changed him, and cared for him in Wasco, a small town about two hours away. She'd thought her love for Jake and her memories of him would fade with the years, but they hadn't. She saw him in Christopher's brown eyes, the quirk of his smile, the beauty of him. She constantly questioned whether she'd done the right thing when she'd left L.A. without telling him about her pregnancy.

With Christopher's first birthday, she'd told herself that Jake had probably gone on with his life. During Christopher's second year, every time she visited her mom in L.A., she'd thought about calling Jake. And this past year as Christopher had learned and grown and asked more questions about the world around him, she'd doubted her decision daily.

A month ago, the owners of the day care facility in Wasco where she'd worked had informed her they'd be closing it at the end of the month. They'd said operating costs were too high and the profit margin not great enough. Thinking about moving back here, she'd sent resumes all over Los Angeles, seriously considering telling Jake they had a son.

Then two weeks ago, she received a phone call from her aunt in the middle of the night, a phone call that had changed her life. Her mother's unexpected death had shaken up Sara's world. It had made her look at her life with Christopher more closely—what he needed. They had Aunt Eloise, her mother's sister. But no one else. Christopher needed his father. Soon he'd begin to ask specific questions. Sara couldn't lie to him. She wanted to tell him what a wonderful man his father was. She wanted him to know Jake because he deserved to know his father. Now, all she had to do was pick up the telephone...

The doorbell rang and Sara jumped. Maybe it was Aunt El. She'd offered to watch Christopher so Sara could start packing her mother's belongings, so she could spend some time alone with her thoughts—in the house where she'd grown up, in the house she'd soon have to vacate.

When she answered the door, a man in a green uniform stood on the porch. "Eloise Murray told me I could find Sara Standish here. I have a package for her."

"I'm Sara Standish."

"Sign here, please."

Sara signed the paper on the clipboard and the young man gave her the manila envelope. She thanked him, closed the door, and checked the letterhead. It was from her mother's lawyer. Sara had met the white-haired, older man when she was a teenager, after her father died.

Slipping her thumb under the flap, she tore the envelope open. Inside, she found a sealed letter along with a note from the lawyer.

Dear Miss Standish,

Your mother instructed me to deliver this letter to you upon her death. I will call you in a few days to set up a time for the reading of her will.

My sincere condolences,

George Gunthry

With shaking fingers, she carefully opened the ivory envelope.

Darling Sara,

I know this will be a difficult time for you. But there is something I'd like you to do. Do you remember your father's gold pocket watch? It's in my jewelry box. I want you to give it to Jake. George made my will after your father died. I preferred not to tamper with it because I want this bequest to be a personal moment between you and Jake. Before Christopher was born, you made a decision considering Jake's wishes. Maybe it's time to consider yours and Christopher's.

I love you, Sara. All I've ever wanted is your happiness. Be happy, sweetheart, no matter what you decide.

Mom

Was this her mother's way of giving her a last bit of guidance, a gentle shove? Making her face Jake again and her feelings for him?

It was time to face the truth, to let Jake decide if he wanted to be a part of his son's life. It was time to let go of the guilt and the doubts and put the decision in his hands.

She would go see him. Test the waters. Tell him about her mother's bequest. Then she'd decide what to do next.

On Wednesday afternoon, the heat of a September sun poured onto Sara's shoulders as she rang Jake's doorbell, praying he still worked from an office in his house. Her courage faded as she stood on the doorstep of the Spanish-styled two-story with its black wrought iron trim and terra cotta-colored exterior. She'd always loved Jake's house with it's old world charm and cozy interior. Was he sharing it with someone else?

The door opened and a pretty woman with light brown hair and a warm smile stood before Sara. Sara was speechless for a moment, though she'd thought about Jake marrying another woman. She swallowed hard, her courage flagging, but her determination taking over.

"Hello? Can I help you?" the woman asked as her gaze slid over Sara's yellow dress and bolero jacket.

"I'm looking for Jake Donovan. Are you...Mrs. Donovan?"

The woman laughed. "Absolutely not." She extended her hand. "I'm Gillian Bradley, and I work with Jake. Are you trying to find someone?"

"Uh, no. Just Jake."

Gillian motioned her to follow. "Come in. He's in the office."

Sara stood in Jake's living room, her emotions tightening her throat. After four long years, everything was the same, from the native American painting above the fireplace to the hand-carved wooden lamps standing as sentinels on either side of the taupe and green tweed sofa. The light wood end tables, their tops inlaid with mosaic tiles, even held the same bronze sculptures of wild horses Jake had purchased from an art collector. She'd stood beside him as he'd bargained for them. The only new piece was a chest with shelves sitting by the stairway.

Gillian motioned to the office, a sunroom adjacent to the living room. Sara walked toward it, her heart pounding.

A portable playpen was set up in one corner. But a child wasn't in it. Jake stood by the windows, holding a toddler. Sara couldn't believe it.

Jake said, "I think Matthew's getting another tooth. I

have an extra teething ring in the refrigerator—" He turned toward the doorway and went perfectly still.

Sara knew she looked different. She'd let her hair grow longer after Christopher was born. She'd lost some weight, too. Working and running after her son had kept her in shape.

But she wasn't the only one who'd changed her hairstyle. Where Jake had once worn his hair cropped short, it now hung to his shirt collar in the back and over his ears on the sides. As for the rest of him— Her heart had already tripled its rhythm. In khakis and a cream polo shirt, he looked good enough to...hug. But the stance of his body, the set expression on his face told her this wasn't a reunion he'd anticipated or ever expected.

Suddenly, the baby waved his arms and reached for Jake's collar. Jake tore his gaze from Sara's and rubbed the little guy's back as if he'd done it many times before. "I think your mom has plans for you."

Gillian laughed. "It's time to go home. He's just trying to coax you into carrying him around a bit longer." She picked up the diaper bag sitting near the playpen, then held out her arms.

Matthew reached for his mother, then swayed back toward Jake with a smile and a gurgle. Jake leaned closer to Gillian. "Go on, pal. I'll see you tomorrow."

Gillian lifted Matthew from Jake's arms. After a short pout, he snuggled in his mom's arm. "Call me if you have any questions on the notes I made. I'll see you in the morning," she said, glancing at Sara, then back to Jake.

Jake nodded, but his gaze returned to Sara's. It wasn't until the front door closed that he finally looked away.

Sara felt shell-shocked, seeing him again. Memories came rushing back along with old feelings. She remembered the day she'd met him, the workshop he'd presented, his intensity when he'd talked about teenagers needing to be guided in the right direction instead of letting them end up in the criminal justice system. After his workshop, she'd approached him with a few questions. They'd gone for coffee and talked, becoming more absorbed in each other than the subject of his presentation. He'd asked her out over the weekend. And their courtship had begun.

She remembered the kisses, the touches, that one special night...

She'd matured and changed over the past four years. Watching Jake hold a child in his arms led her to believe he'd changed, too.

Her memories and emotions kept her immobilized. Jake had to pass her to get to his desk chair. When he did, she could have sworn they both held their breath. The brief contact of his shoulder against hers as he by-passed the playpen acted like a jolt of electricity to her already overloaded nervous system.

Not knowing where to start, she said, "Gillian said she was your partner."

"Yes, she is."

"She brings her baby to work?"

Jake lodged one hip against the desk. "Sometimes."

"How old is...Matthew, isn't it?"

"Fifteen months." The lines along Jake's mouth that carved into his lean cheeks when he smiled now looked deeper than they had four years ago.

Sara couldn't keep the burning question in her mind. "Is Matthew yours?"

Jake looked as though he might not answer, but then in a brisk tone explained, "Gillian is happily married to a friend of mine. Matthew is theirs."

"I was surprised to see you with a child."

"I never said I didn't like kids. I just didn't want to bring any into the world."

When the silence stretched into an unbearable awkwardness, he asked, "Why are you here?"

There was no welcome in his voice, none of the gentleness she knew he was capable of. The wall he'd erected the last time they'd talked, the day he'd left her mother's house, was solid and sturdy. All she could do was take one step at a time.

"My mother passed away two weeks ago." Sara's throat tightened and she had to fight back the tears that were all too ready to come to the surface these days.

Jake's stony expression softened. "I'm sorry. I know how much she meant to you."

Yes, he did. In fact, he'd known everything about her because she'd held nothing back. Not until she'd received the news of her pregnancy. "I've been staying at Aunt El's."

"How's your aunt taking this?" he asked, his tone bringing back memories of his arms around her, confidences shared, yellow roses.

She shook off the images and the feelings that went with them to concentrate on his question. Her Aunt Eloise and her mother had been close all their lives. "It's difficult for her."

Jake stuffed his hands into his pockets, a familiar gesture. He always did it when he was uncomfortable. "I am sorry about your mother, but you could have sent me a note. Why did you come?" He seemed genuinely perplexed.

"Because Mom left me a letter. She wants you to have something of my dad's."

The seconds ticked by. "Why?"

"Because she liked you, Jake. She...she just wanted you to have it." Sara knew Jake's memories of his mother weren't all happy ones, that's why she'd hoped he could share her mother. It was too late. But it wasn't too late for him to have a relationship with his son. "I wanted to invite you over to Mom's house to pick it up. How about tomorrow sometime?"

Jake looked torn. Finally, he said, "All right. Around one?"

"That's fine. I'll look forward to seeing you then."

He pushed away from his desk. "I'll walk you out."

Jake felt almost numb and didn't try to make conversation as he walked Sara Standish to the door. He'd never expected to see her again. He'd told himself she was history. But he couldn't look at a yellow rose, he couldn't close his eyes sometimes, he couldn't look at the tux still hanging in his closet without wondering what they could have had, without wondering why he still missed her, without wondering if she was now married to someone else, mothering the children she'd wanted.

The sense of betrayal he'd experienced when she'd called off the wedding had never ebbed. He'd fallen in love with her and he'd trusted her—with his heart and with his life. But he hadn't been enough for her. His love hadn't been enough. She'd wanted more. She'd wanted something he couldn't give her because in giving her a child, he would have given himself unending heartache. His grief over his dead son hadn't lessened, it had taken a deeper foothold. Sara's broken promise had made him more guarded, and he knew he'd built an impenetrable shell around his heart.

So why did Sara's presence in his house make that shell feel not quite as secure, as if it needed another layer?

Jake glanced at her again. If he looked too hard, too long, he might feel something that after she left again could only hurt him more. She was so damn pretty. Those big blue eyes once filled with optimism and sparkling enthusiasm now reflected sadness and something else he couldn't put his finger on. But it didn't matter. After tomorrow he'd never see her again.

He opened the door for her. When she stepped over the threshold onto the porch, he called, "Sara?"

She turned.

"Don't go to any trouble tomorrow. I won't be able to stay. I have appointments later in the afternoon."

As soon as he saw her disappointment, he regretted his abrupt words. She looked as if she was about to say something, but then changed her mind. Instead, she nodded. "I'll see you tomorrow around one."

Jake watched her walk down the path to her car, wishing he could deny her effect on him, wishing tomorrow over so feelings he'd kept in check for four years could stay buried.

Jake walked up the steps to the house Jennie Standish had rented, remembering the last time he'd left it the night Sara had called off their wedding.

He'd thought he was over her. He'd thought he'd gone on with his life. But just one look at her, the scent of her, the lift of her brow when she was unsure, was enough to make every nerve in his body need. And not just any woman, but her. He hadn't slept last night. Not that insomnia was new to him. But too many memories had come crashing back.

When he rang the doorbell, Sara answered immediately. She must have been waiting. She was dressed in a navy top and shorts that wasn't intentionally seductive, but showed off her slim figure. Had she lost weight? He'd always liked her short hair, but he had to admit the longer style was sensually enticing. He wanted to touch it, to brush her cheek, to—

He gave himself a mental kick.

"Come in," she said softly.

That damn soft voice. He'd never heard it raised in anger. "I can't stay long." He knew he was curt, but he had to watch every response, every syllable, every thought.

She led him to the living room couch. He chose a side chair. Not commenting, she lifted a small felt pouch from the coffee table. "This is what Mom wanted you to have."

Her fingers brushed his palm and the years slipped away. Heat forked through him and he remembered the night they'd made love. He'd never forget that night as long as he lived—the intimacy, the closeness, the sheer pleasure.

Focusing on the pouch, he opened it and shook the contents into his hand. A gold watch. Her father's watch. A lump formed in Jake's throat.

"Sara, I don't know what to say."

"You don't have to say anything. I think Mom had a reason for giving that to you."

He heard the seriousness in Sara's voice and his investigative senses went on alert. More was going on here than a bequest. Sara had come back into his life for some reason. "Why did she give it to me?"

He watched Sara's breasts rise and fall as she took a deep breath. "I've been living in Wasco, Jake. When Mom died, I wasn't with her. It was a heart attack, out of the blue..." Her words faded and she blinked away emotion.

He wanted to comfort her, but he knew better and stayed put. "Sara?"

She regained her composure. "When Mom died, I had to rethink decisions I'd made. Decisions that involved you."

He cocked his head and listened intently, to hear what she wasn't saying. "Go on."

"I felt it was best at the time. I thought— Well, it doesn't matter what I thought. The last four years I've been doubting my decision. Since Mom died, I realized I was wrong and you need to know."

"What do I need to know?" He asked the question slowly, expecting a shock, trying to prepare himself for whatever was coming.

"You have a son. I was pregnant the night I called off the wedding."

The buzz of a lawn mower penetrated the windows. The space between him and Sara vibrated with his shock and something much stronger than that came from his gut and surged through his bloodstream.

Sara's hands fluttered. "I couldn't tell you. I didn't want you to marry me for that reason, not when you didn't want children. I couldn't see any other way to go."

He could hardly contain his anger, his sense of betrayal, and he felt like a volcano ready to blow. "You could have told me the truth!"

"No, I couldn't have. Because you would have done the honorable thing despite the way you felt, and that would have been wrong for both of us."

He'd never imagined Sara could lie or deceive. He'd trusted her and this was how she'd repaid that trust. Anger rushed through him, vibrating in his quick response. "So you did the dishonorable thing. You lied," he added, his voice sharp and meant to cut through her.

"I didn't lie. I told you I wanted children. I wanted this baby. I never could have given him up for adoption or—"

Jake leaned forward, his arms braced on his knees, his breathing fast, his heart pounding. "Don't say it. I can't believe you believed I'd want you to do either. Not after what we shared." He remembered her telling him she loved him. He remembered loving her.

Her voice quivered. "You didn't want children!"

He straightened and tried to rein in his reaction so he could think clearly, so he could get the information he needed. "No, I didn't. But once you found out you were pregnant, I had a right to know. What's his name?"

"Christopher," she said quietly.

Pictures of Davie flashed in Jake's mind. Every one of them hurt to see. "Where is he?"

"Right now he's with Aunt Eloise...at her house. We'll be staying with her as I empty this one."

"I want to see him. **Now**." He was prepared for any argument she might give to keep him away from his son.

To his surprise, she didn't argue. Rather she said, "I would have brought him with me but I didn't know if you'd have to think about this—"

"There's nothing to think about." He stood. "Let's go. I remember where your aunt lives. I'll follow you." He wouldn't let Sara out of his sight until he saw his son. And then... One step at a time.

Sara felt shaken to her core as she locked the door and they went to their cars. She wished she could say something to cut the tension between them, to diffuse Jake's anger. But she realized she had to let it wear off...she had to be patient. And she would be patient as long as it took. Because she still loved this man.

She always would.

When she pulled into the driveway of her aunt's house, she took a few deep breaths. She had no idea what Jake's reaction would be when he saw his son, but she'd soon find out. She didn't wait for Jake but went to the door, opened it, and called to her aunt. "I'm back."

"In the kitchen," her aunt responded. "Cookie time."

Jake's car screeched to a stop in front of the house. He ran up to the porch and came in behind her.

"Christopher's in the kitchen with Aunt El."

Jake grasped Sara's arm. "Does he know?"

"What?"

"Will he know I'm his father?"

"No. I haven't talked to him about it yet because I wasn't sure what you'd want to do."

He released her, but the heat from his skin remained. "Introduce me as his father. That's what I am. That's what I'll always be."

Lord, she wished she had a child psychologist at her elbow. She supposed the best thing to do was to be honest with her son in the simplest way possible. "Give me a few minutes to explain to him."

Jake searched her face, his eyes probing, anger still in evidence. "That's probably best for him. I'll wait here."

Sara breathed a sigh of relief and went to the kitchen. Her Aunt Eloise stood at the counter mixing a meat loaf. "I saw Jake get out of his car."

"As soon as I told him, he insisted on coming over."

Eloise smiled. "Good."

Christopher was eating a cookie. Sara crossed to him and sat beside him. "Hi, honey. How was your morning?"

He took another bite of the cookie. "Okay."

"I need to talk to you about something."

Christopher kept munching.

"Remember when you asked me if you had a daddy, I said you did but he lived somewhere else?"

Her son nodded.

"What would you think about meeting your dad?"

Christopher's eyes brightened and he smiled. "A daddy like Patti's?"

Patti was one of Christopher's friends from day care. Her father had picked her up every day. "He's your dad so he wouldn't be exactly like Patti's. He's is the living room. Should I get him?"

Christopher nodded and put the cookie on the table.

Sara returned to the living room and saw Jake pacing back and forth. "He's looking forward to meeting you." It sounded so formal. But what else could she say? She didn't know what was going to happen any more than Jake did as he followed her to the kitchen.

"Hello, Jake," Eloise said simply. Her aunt had invited her and Jake to dinner a few times when they were engaged.

Jake nodded, but his attention was all on his son.

Sara went over to her three-year-old, who was still munching on his cookie. She laid her hand on top of his head and ruffled his black hair. "Honey, this is your daddy."

Her son looked up at her with wide brown eyes. Sara swallowed hard. "Jake, this is Christopher."

Jake approached slowly, as if he couldn't believe the three-year-old in front of his eyes. The lines deepened around his mouth and his quick intake of breath told her he was remembering another little boy, another son. The pain on his face was almost more than she could stand. Would seeing Christopher always bring him pain? How would that pain affect his relationship with Christopher and with her?

Jake crouched down beside his son and glanced at the pile of crumbs in front of him. "I guess you like chocolate chip cookies."

"Mommy's an' Auntie El's."

"I know your mommy can make a great chocolate chip cookie. How many have you had?"

Christopher looked up at Sara then leaned closer to Jake and held up three fingers. "I eat two."

Jake smiled.

Christopher took a cookie from the plate in the middle of the table and offered it to Jake. "Want one?"

Jake's smile faded as he took the cookie and stood, leaning against the table as he took a bite. From experience, Sara knew he was reining in emotions, thinking, letting logic decide his next step.

Finally he said to Christopher, "Maybe you and I could go outside and take a walk in the back yard. What do you think?"

Christopher looked up at Sara. Trying to protect her son but wanting to give Jake every opening she could, she asked Christopher, "Do you want to?"

Her son examined Jake from his six-one stature, over his face, to his sneakers. "Okay." Checking with his mother again, he asked, "Is he a stranger?"

Sara glanced at Jake—the curling black hair at his throat where two buttons stood open, his taut stomach, his long legs and tanned arms, and she took another deep breath. "No, he's not a stranger." She and her son had talked many times about not playing or speaking with people he didn't know unless she was there. Daddy or not, he didn't know Jake.

Jake's gaze met hers briefly. She felt the shock of it to her toes, anger mixed with anguish, and accusation. Taking a towel from the handle of the oven, she wiped her son's mouth and hands, then brushed her hand across his hair once more. "Maybe you can show your daddy the pretty rocks you found."

Christopher jumped from his chair and went to the door. "See rocks?"

Jake followed his son. "Sure."

Christopher chattered about where he'd found his treasures, his voice fading as they walked down the yard.

Eloise put her arm around her niece's shoulders. "It'll work out, dear. You'll see."

"He's angry with me, Aunt El."

Her aunt patted her shoulder. "Of course, he is. He has a right to be."

Sara thought about it as she had a million times before. "I couldn't marry him. It would have been wrong. But I should have stood my ground, not married him, and then told him about the baby."

Eloise dropped her arm and went to peer out the door at Jake and her great nephew. "You were young, Sara. Jake was ten years older and a strong-minded man. If he'd insisted on marriage, I'm not sure you could have held out against him."

To see Christopher walk beside Jake gave Sara great joy. To watch Jake take his son's hand also caused her great sadness because she'd kept them apart. How could she ever make up for that? Her aunt's words penetrated.

Could she have held out against Jake if he'd wanted marriage anyway back then? "I don't know. Maybe that's why I did it the way I did. But I do know I'm going to move back here and give Jake as much time as he wants with Christopher. I owe him that."

"You don't know what kind of father he'll be."

"I think I do. Just look at them."

Father and son hunkered down over a pile of rocks. Christopher pointed out something.

"The novelty might wear off."

Sara knew her aunt was playing devil's advocate. "No. Jake's not that type of man. He doesn't pretend what he doesn't feel."

Eloise faced her niece. "Do you think he'll be staying for supper?"

"I have no idea, Aunt El. I have no idea what Jake's going to do. I'll have to wait and see."

Sitting in the sun on the warm grass beside Christopher, Jake couldn't help staring at the boy. He looked so much like Davie. His features—Jake's features. His eyes—Jake's eyes. Had Christopher looked like Davie as an infant, as a one-year-old? How old was he when he cut his first tooth, said his first word, took his first step?

Jake still couldn't believe Sara had lied to him, left him, and cheated him out of three years with his son. Finding it hard to absorb, fighting off the dark anger he didn't want to influence his attitude toward Christopher, he suddenly felt the immensity of the responsibility that had fallen on him out of nowhere. Without warning, or time to prepare, he was a father again. This time he had to do it right. This time he had to make sure his son was safe every minute of every day. He didn't want to let the boy out of his sight. Yet he knew he had to temper his fears.

What was Sara planning? Why had she told him now? Was she willing to move back to L.A.? Would she let him be a parent? She had no choice. No matter where she lived, Christopher was Jake's son and he'd get to know his child one way or another. The problem was—how was he going to handle having Sara back in his life?

The way he handled everything else...very carefully.

"Look, Daddy."

The sound of the title, the childlike quality of Christopher's voice, tore Jake apart. Because he remembered another time, another voice. Yet when Christopher handed him the gray stone and his small fingers touched Jake's palm, Jake felt the pride of fatherhood again. Yes, this time he would do it right.

A half hour later, when Jake and his son returned to the kitchen, Christopher ran to his mother. "Milk, Mommy? Daddy drinks milk, too!"

Sara's gaze met Jake's with uncertainty. The fact of the matter was that he felt such confusion about Sara right now, he knew he needed time away from her and Christopher so he could think, and plan, and decide the best route to take. He certainly didn't trust her. He might never be able to trust her again.

She went to the refrigerator and opened the door, pulling out the milk carton. "Jake, would you like to stay for a while, maybe for dinner?"

Jake looked at Christopher and then back at her. "No. I have to get back. I left some work unfinished." He turned to his son. "But I'll see you again. Soon." He ruffled Christopher's hair. "We can have milk and cookies together next time. Okay?"

Christopher bobbed his head enthusiastically.

Sara waited for the three-year-old to sit at the table, then she poured him a glass of milk. "I'll be right at the front door. Aunt El's in her sewing room. If you go in there with her, don't touch anything unless she says you can."

Jake had trouble tearing himself away from Christopher, putting physical distance between them. After a last long look, he walked to the front door. Sara stood a few feet from him.

His voice was gruff with all the unsaid thoughts and feelings churning inside him. "Are you going back to Wasco?"

She straightened her shoulders and tilted up her chin, looking directly into his eyes. "What do you want, Jake?"

The question she should have asked four years ago intensified the churning in his gut, and he couldn't keep the anger at bay. "So now you're going to think about that?"

"I've always thought about what you wanted and didn't want."

She was lying. She couldn't have thought about him and still kept Christopher away for so long. Silence stretched between them until he said in a low tone, "I need time to think. Just don't go running off without telling me. Because if you do—"

She didn't let him finish his warning. "I won't. Do you want to spend time with Christopher tomorrow?"

Could he believe she wouldn't run? Could he believe she'd stay at least until they made some decisions? He looked into the kitchen where his son was still drinking his milk. "I'll call you."

And with that, Jake stepped onto the porch and closed the door behind him, in more turmoil than he'd experienced in years.

Chapter Two

Jake strode into his office, expecting to be alone. But Gillian was still there, sitting at her desk, sorting through mail. "You missed your appointment with Mrs. Johnson. I took down the information and told her you'd call her."

"Damn! I forgot."

"You don't forget appointments, Jake. What's going on?"

Jake walked over to Gillian's son who was sleeping peacefully in the portable playpen. He couldn't begin to sort out his feelings for himself, let alone tell Gillian about them. In his mind he saw Christopher as he'd sat playing in the sun. Pain sliced through him again.

"Jake? What's wrong?" Gillian's voice was worried.

Though Gillian had psychic powers that helped her find missing persons, she used her intuition more than she used her "gift" to tune into people. That's why their partnership as private investigators worked so well. Her intuition matched with his skill, logic and contacts could find almost anybody. That's what he did now—he found people. He didn't get in the middle of divorces or track down thieves anymore.

Gillian was waiting for an answer, and he knew she wouldn't let him evade her. Of course, that was the down side of their partnership, sometimes she was too intuitive. "Sara and I...have a history."

"This room sizzled yesterday with whatever is between the two of you."

Jake went to the window and stared outside. "She walked out on our wedding because I didn't want kids. Today, she told me we have one. He's three plus a few months and his name is Christopher." Jake had told few people about his background, but Gillian and her husband Nathan knew about his childhood, Mary Beth and Davie. He'd never told them about Sara.

"What are you going to do?"

He ran his hand through his hair. "That's the million dollar question. I just met him. He's great. Intelligent, friendly, curious..."

"His mother probably had a lot to do with that."

Jake scowled. "Maybe. But every time I look at him..." He swore. "This is why I didn't want more kids. How can I protect him, keep him safe, give him everything he needs—"

"How does Sara feel about you spending time with him?"

Jake tried to shove away the anger and the ache in his heart whenever he pictured Sara so he could think more clearly. Sinking into his desk chair, he wheeled to face Gillian. "You know, you ask a lot of questions."

Gillian put down the letters. "You know, I care."

He could be himself with Gillian and her husband. And they did care about him. "I haven't thought about all the questions, let alone the answers. How would you feel if you were just told you had a son and you'd missed the first three years of his life?"

"Angry. Rattled. Confused."

Jake rocked back and forth on the springs. "Yeah. All three. Plus. Except I know one thing. I'm not going to lose him like I lost Davie. I just have to figure out the best way to deal with all this."

"What about his mother?"

Jake stopped rocking. "What about her?"

"What do you feel?"

He stood and paced the office. "Mad! She ran out on me. She lied to me. And yet when I look at her..." He stopped pacing and more to himself than to Gillian, he muttered, "I still get turned inside out."

"You don't have to take on the problems of the world by yourself, you know. Nathan and I are here if you want to talk."

"That's not my style."

"You might have to change your style to handle this one."

Jake's mind buzzed with scrambled pictures from the past—Mary Beth and Davie, the first day he'd met Sara on the college campus where he was giving a seminar on teenagers and the criminal justice system, the day she'd agreed to marry him, the night she'd called it off. All of it still hurt. Too damn much. There was no way he could begin to talk about it, not even with Gillian and Nathan.

And Sara...

No matter what happened with Christopher, he'd protect himself this time. He wouldn't let her in. He wouldn't give her the chance to hurt him again.

Cutting sandwiches into halves, Sara stacked them on a plate. When she glanced up at the kitchen clock, her heart beat faster. Jake would be stopping by soon. Usually they'd finished lunch by the time he arrived to play with Christopher, but she'd spent the morning at her mother's trying to pack up the dining room.

Every day for a week, Jake had visited his son, playing with him, building with blocks, digging in the soil making mud pies. He tried hard to hide his thoughts, but Sara could see the strain on his face...in his body language. She knew he was remembering Davie. She knew he resented her. But instead of putting it into words, he was keeping it inside. She wanted to help him, but he wouldn't let her get close. Their conversations were superficial, the tension between them always simmering. She kept telling herself that she was prepared for his anger, but part of her kept hoping he'd understand and forgive her.

Expecting him, she'd left the front door open. When Jake rang the bell, she called, "Come in."

He entered the kitchen, his jeans, T-shirt and rakish hair enhancing his rugged male appeal. "You shouldn't let just anybody wander in."

"I knew you'd be coming."

"This isn't Wasco, Sara."

She sighed. "I know that. I grew up here, remember?" One look into his eyes told her he remembered other things, too. "I'm sorry Christopher's not ready. We didn't have lunch yet. We were over at Mom's, packing up."

"How's it going?"

"Slowly. It's hard."

"I could have come by this evening instead."

"No, this is fine. It's difficult for me to be there very long."

"Is there anything I can do to help?"

She stopped spreading mustard on the bread and faced him. He wasn't offering out of politeness. Maybe he did have some feelings left. If he did, they could build on those. "Not at this stage. I have to do a lot of sorting. I did want to ask you if you could possibly come a little later tomorrow and watch Christopher for me."

Her heart beat faster as he came to the counter where she was standing.

"Do you and Eloise want to spend the afternoon at your mom's?"

"No. Aunt El and I have to go to the reading of Mom's will. It shouldn't take long, an hour if that. I can take Christopher along, but if you'd like to spend time with him, I can ask him if he wants to stay with you."

Jake stared at the plate of sandwiches for a moment. "Is that what you want? Or would you like me to come along?"

"You'd do that?"

Jake shrugged. "I'm Christopher's father. I thought there might be good reason for me to sit in."

She should have known he wouldn't be going just to give her moral support. "Of course, I should have thought of that. Christopher can take his coloring book. That should occupy him. My appointment is at two."

"Two should be fine. Gillian will be in the office tomorrow."

Now that they were talking, she had to tell him about her plans. "I wanted to tell you—I'll be moving back to L.A. I've sent resumes to every day care center in the area."

"What about your life in Wasco? You can leave it that easily?"

She thought he looked relieved about her decision, but it was hard to tell. "About a month ago, I'd decided to look for a job in L.A. The day care center where I worked closed and I had to make a change anyway. I was trying to get up the courage to tell you about Christopher when Mom died."

Jake shifted against the counter and his arm brushed hers. "So I'll be able to see Christopher whenever I want."

It wasn't a question, but a challenge. "You can see him whenever you want...*within reason.*"

He looked as if he hadn't expected her to stand up to him. But she wouldn't let her guilt override what was best for their son.

"And who's going to decided what's within reason?" he asked blandly, though his eyes had darkened.

"We'll have to compromise or let Aunt Eloise be the judge. She'd be fair."

He was standing so close that she could catch the scent of his aftershave, trace his shoulder muscles in the worn T-shirt. For a moment she thought she saw respect in his eyes if nothing else, and in that same moment, she thought he leaned closer.

Then, like a bolt of thunder startling her, the back door opened and Christopher scrambled in. "Is lunch ready?"

Jake stepped away, his expression unreadable. Sara felt shut out again and was left with an emptiness she'd known for far too long.

After reading Jennifer Standish's will, George Gunthry laid it on the blotter in front of him and summed it up. "In essence, Jennie's personal effects as well as the proceeds of the property she owned in Arizona go to Sara. Do any of you have any questions?"

Sara's mom and dad had bought the property in Arizona, thinking it a good investment for their later years, hoping the value of it would soar.

Jake shifted in the straight-back chair beside Sara's.

On Sara's other side, her aunt asked, "So what do you suggest we do first, Mr. Gunthry? How long does my niece have before she has to vacate the house?"

The white-haired lawyer responded kindly. "Spend some time in the house sorting through Jennie's things. Decide what you'd like to keep. I suggest we call an auctioneer for the rest. Because Jennie rented from Mr. Hale for so long, he's giving you until the end of October to vacate."

Sara tightened her hand around her purse. "It will be difficult auctioning furniture I've seen my mother use all her life."

"Would you rather keep it?" the lawyer asked.

"I have to find a job and rent a place for us. I don't know if I can do that in a month."

Her aunt asked the lawyer. "What if she'd rent her mother's house?"

Sara shook her head. "It's too big. We don't need that much room. Besides, I can't rent anything until I find a job."

Jake shifted again and asked, "How soon would you have to set up the auction?"

"That depends on Sara," Gunthry responded.

"I'll need a week or two to decide..." Sara's voice trailed off as she thought about it.

"I'm afraid that's all the time you have, Sara, unless you want to put the furniture in storage. Let me know by October first, all right? That way we can set up the auction and advertise it."

Christopher, who was sitting at Sara's feet with his coloring book, tugged at her hand. "Look, Mommy."

She smiled at her son. "That's nice, honey."

He tugged at her hand again. "Mommy..."

Jake crooked his finger at the little boy. "Come here and show me. Your Mom's trying to talk to Mr. Gunthry."

Both Sara's and Christopher's heads swung toward Jake. It seemed strange having someone else directing her son. But if Christopher was going to see Jake as his father, she had to back him. "Show your dad and I'll look at the pictures later."

Christopher's lip sagged in a pout until Jake held out his arms, then Christopher crawled onto his father's lap and pointed to the picture he'd just colored. The two of them were definitely forming a bond.

Sara realized she had to get on with her life, not look toward the past. "I'll make up my mind soon. You'll take care of the property in Arizona?"

"I'll research the real estate companies in the area and find the most competent one. But it could take a while to sell it with the market the way it is. From what I understand, it's in a remote area." He paused. "Do you have any other questions?"

"Not now," Sara answered.

While Eloise asked the attorney a question about inheritance tax, Jake leaned toward Sara, his arm brushing hers. "What is the property in Arizona?"

"Just a little plot of land Mom and Dad bought because they thought it would increase in value for their retirement. But it's in the middle of nowhere and I doubt if it has." Her throat tightened. This appointment had been difficult for her. The reading of the will made everything seem more final. She'd lost both of her parents and hanging onto their possessions wouldn't help. She'd just have to hold onto them with her heart. If she only had a short time to make decisions, she'd better get busy.

"Jake, would it be all right if you saw Christopher tomorrow evening? I'm going to spend the day at Mom's."

He searched her face, then nodded. "No problem."

Where their son was concerned, they didn't have a problem. At least not yet. But from Jake's pensive expression, she wondered if they might not have a problem soon.

The next afternoon, Sara laid her mother's clothes in piles, sorting the casual everyday slacks and tops from the dresses her mother had worn to church. Eloise had insisted Sara go through her mother's personal effects herself while she worked in the kitchen and kept Christopher occupied.

Sara was buttoning a blazer when she heard footsteps on the stairs and knew instantly they were Jake's. Why was he here? After the reading of the will, he'd been quiet. He'd given Christopher a hug outside the lawyer's office and told Sara he'd see her this evening.

Jake came into the bedroom. His navy shorts, red polo shirt and sneakers made him look more like a tennis coach than a PI. Although she could feel his gaze on her, she positioned the blazer on top of the other clothes and returned to the closet, removing a handful of dresses.

"How's it going?" he asked gently.

"Fine."

"Christopher looked as busy as your aunt. He's helping her empty the kitchen cabinets."

Sara could still see her mother cooking in that kitchen, still almost smell the pumpkin bread and apple pie that were her specialties. She spoke past the lump in her throat. "Helping?"

Jake chuckled. "He was using two lids as cymbals."

Sara put one of her mother's dresses on the pile on the bed. "Maybe I should bring him up here for a while and give Aunt El a break."

"Maybe *you* should take a break. Eloise said you've been at this since nine o'clock this morning. It's almost two."

"I took a break for lunch." She gazed at a green and white print dress that was one of her mother's favorites.

Jake crossed to the middle of the room where three cardboard boxes stood, one with purses, one with shoes, one with odds and ends. "Sara, you don't have to do this all in one day."

"It won't get any easier. I just have to do it." She laid the green and white dress with the others. "Did you need something? I mean since you came over?"

"No. I thought I could take Christopher to the playground so you and your aunt can work uninterrupted."

Jake's unexpected appearance and kindness was more than Sara could handle at that moment. The ice blue suit of her mother's she held in her hand had been special. She had helped her mother pick it out. Jennie Standish had worn it for her twentieth wedding anniversary the year before she'd lost her husband.

Suddenly, the immensity of Sara's loss shook her. She couldn't keep her chin from quivering as her eyes filled with tears. This time she couldn't stop them. Turning toward the closet, she hoped Jake wouldn't see.

"Do you think Christopher will go with me without you?"

All she could do was nod as she tried to swallow a sob.

"Sara?"

She managed, "I'm sure he'll—"

The hand on her shoulder stopped her pretense. Jake nudged her around and saw the tears coursing down her cheeks. "What's wrong?" he asked so gently her tears flowed freer.

"I miss Mom so much. And Dad. It's like I lost him all over again. I can't believe they're both gone." Her shoulders shook, and she bowed her head.

Blessedly she felt Jake's arms around her, and she sobbed into his chest. He held her close, and she cried as she hadn't been able to since her aunt notified her of her mother's death.

Jake didn't say anything, and she was thankful because there was nothing anyone could say. The loss was too fresh, the pain too sharp for words to comfort. But the warmth of Jake's body against hers and the strength of his arms did comfort. They stood that way a long time, her cheek and hands pressed to his chest. The feel and smell of him were familiar, awakening more than comfort, reminding her of the night they'd shared.

The beat of his heart, strong and rhythmic, hastened under her hand. His heat surrounded her, becoming steamier the longer they stood together. His muscles grew taut, and she could feel tension spread through him.

He pulled away and she felt cold and alone...alone enough to look up at him with the longing she felt. His jaw tightened, and he took another step back. She saw his chest rise and fall as he pulled a long draught of air into his lungs. The next instant his expression was set, control and restraint evident in the straightness of his shoulders, the rigidity of his stance.

The same control made his voice even. "I'll send Christopher up so you can talk to him about going with me."

Just as quickly as Jake had entered the room, he'd disappeared.

Sara pulled in a few deep breaths of her own. Taking a tissue from the box on the dresser, she blew her nose. The tension between her and Jake was getting worse instead of better, and she didn't know what to begin to do about it.

Three weeks had passed. Sara pushed a carton aside with her foot as she readied her mother's belongings for public auction. Just last week, she'd gone to two preliminary job interviews. But she hadn't heard anything yet. She had some savings, but not enough to put her mother's furniture in storage. So she'd had no choice but to go ahead with the auction. Without a job, she couldn't rent an apartment. Eloise was insisting she and Christopher could stay with her as long as they needed to. But Sara had always been independent. She'd raised Christopher on her own, and she wanted them to be on their own now. But until she found a job, that wasn't possible.

Many days during the past three weeks, Jake had come to entertain Christopher so Eloise and Sara could work without distraction. Sara had thanked him often, but he didn't seem to want her thanks. He didn't seem to want anything from her except time with their son.

Two days she'd gone back to Wasco, packed up her apartment, closed it, and left the boxes she couldn't fit into her car with the apartment manager. She'd taken Christopher along and Jake hadn't protested. He seemed to think about what was best for Christopher as much as she did. He'd realized Christopher needed to say goodbye to Wasco, too. Today, the day before the auction, Jake had offered to help with the heavy work. Between watching Christopher and dealing with memories associated with her mother's possessions, Sara hadn't had time to think about herself and Jake...at least not this morning.

She opened the upstairs hall closet. It seemed empty, but she knew she should check the back of the top shelf. She found a stepstool in one of the bedrooms and climbed up. A large shoebox zigzagged across the back corner. Leaning forward, she tried to catch the lip with her finger. She'd managed to snag it when the stepstool tilted. The next thing she knew the box had spilled over the shelf, and Jake had swept her into his arms.

Her heart raced and her throat went dry. He'd discarded the cotton shirt he'd worn with his jeans. The muscle shirt he'd worn underneath left nothing to her imagination—not his muscles, not his tanned skin, not the springy hair tickling her arm.

"You should be more careful." His husky voice fell over her, and although it was October, she felt as hot as she would in August.

"I will be," she squeaked, aware of the rise and fall of his chest, his heart speeding with hers. Clearing her throat, she tried again. "I'll put the phone book on the stool."

He arched his brows and grimaced. "Oh, that's real careful," he drawled as he set her on her feet.

"I have to finish emptying everything."

"So call if you need help."

"I don't want to take advantage of your help."

Jake's brown eyes held her for an interminably long moment. "I'll let you know if I think you're taking advantage."

She knew he would. Maybe she was afraid to put any pressure on their relationship, any more than was already there.

Jake mounted the stool, lifted the box, and with his other hand, scooped up the contents that had spilled out. Jumping off the stool, he laid the papers on the top step. One of the photographs floated to the carpet.

Sara picked it up, recognizing it immediately. It was a picture of her and Jake her mom had taken the day they'd become engaged. Had she subconsciously left this box for last? She knew what else was in it. Her gaze went to the stepstool the same time as Jake's. A wedding invitation lay there. Their wedding invitation.

Venturing into frozen territory, Sara laid the photograph on top of the invitation. "The night I called off the wedding—"

"Sara, this won't do any good."

"Please let me tell you, Jake. It might help you understand."

When he remained silent, she took that as a sign he'd listen. "That night when I came in, I heard you and Mom. The doctor had just told me I was pregnant. I heard Mom ask you why you felt the way you did about children. Your response was so vehement, so absolute, that I knew if you couldn't accept children, I couldn't marry you."

"You didn't tell me you were carrying our child."

"But, Jake..."

"Like I said, Sara. This won't do any good." He glanced at the shelf in the closet. "There's nothing else up there. If you need any more help, I'll be downstairs."

She needed Jake. She needed him to open his heart to her as he'd opened it to his son.

A short while later, Sara heard the telephone ring downstairs. She'd unplugged the phone in her mother's bedroom. From the foot of the stairs, Jake called, "Sara, it's for you."

She couldn't imagine who would be calling her unless it was Mr. Gunthry. "I'm coming."

She hurried down the stairs. Before she lifted the receiver to her ear, Jake said, "It's a guy named Mark."

Sara smiled. Mark was a good friend and had been her next door apartment neighbor. She'd given him all the numbers where he could reach her since her cell phone wasn't always reliable holding a charge. Sinking down on the floor where the phone lay, she crossed her legs under her.

Jake was almost finished removing furniture from the living room to the garage. All that remained were the end tables and coffee table. He concentrated on them now, making sure nothing was left in the small drawers. He listened, not feeling guilty in the least. The past few weeks, he'd felt as if his life had been turned upside down. The more he saw Christopher, the more time he wanted to spend with him. Each time he left his son, he didn't like the feeling.

There was only one solution to not leaving Christopher...having Christopher live with him. Yet he couldn't take a child from his mother. Besides, there were no grounds. From what Jake could see, Christopher came first with Sara. Always.

Of course, there was another solution. He could marry Sara. After all, she'd taken care of their son and from what he could tell had done a very good job. She'd raised him alone and Jake knew that couldn't have been easy. On the other hand, at any time she could have called him. Why hadn't she?

He wondered about her decision to stay in L.A. Was she doing it for herself, for him, for Christopher? Was she staying out of guilt? Where Sara was concerned, there were too many questions and not enough answers. Because he didn't know if he could believe what she told him. He didn't know if he could believe her about anything important ever again.

The problem was that whenever he came within two feet of her...

"Hi, Mark. I meant to call but things have been hectic. Thanksgiving? I hope to get back sooner than that to pick up the boxes I left with Mr. Jenkins." She glanced sideways at Jake as if she wished he weren't within hearing distance.

Tough. He was staying. Sara had driven back to Wasco twice, returning with carfuls both times. The boxes were stacked in Eloise's garage. Sara had taken Christopher to Wasco with her. Those were the only two days Jake had missed seeing his son since he'd learned he had one. Now, he wondered how much time Sara had spent with this man named Mark.

"No, I know we didn't have much since it was furnished," Sara said. "I left a few boxes I couldn't fit into

the car. Mr. Jenkins was great. He pro-rated the month."
She listened for a moment. "If you could do that, it
would save me another trip up. I'll send you a money
order so you can ship them. You have my aunt's ad-
dress?" She smiled and listened again.

"Christopher is fine. He hasn't mentioned yet what
he wants for Christmas. A fire engine? I'm sure he'd love
it. I've been trying to get Mom's estate in order but now
I'll concentrate on him and the holidays... Sure you can
talk to him. Hold on." She cupped her hand over the
receiver. "Christopher. Mark wants to tell you something."

Jake watched his son run to the phone, eager to talk
to the man on the other end of the line. While Sara
looked on, Christopher chattered to Mark about his
aunt, the ice cream cone he had yesterday and finally
said, "I have a Daddy now." He held out the receiver to
his mother.

Sara took the phone. "Yes, I did. I wasn't going to get
into that now." She glanced up at Jake. "Yes, everything's
fine. I'll write or call when we're more settled."

After a few more minutes of conversation, she hung
up. Christopher ran back to the kitchen to be with
Eloise and Jake asked, "Who's Mark?"

Sara rose from the floor. "He was a neighbor...and
friend."

"How much of a friend?"

"He's going to send the few remaining boxes so I
don't have to drive back up."

"Have you known him long?"

"Ever since I moved to Wasco."

"He's not married, I take it."

"No. Divorced."

"Were you ever lovers?" Jake figured if he shocked her, she'd tell him the truth.

Totally astonished, Sara just gaped at Jake. As the astonishment wore off, annoyance took its place. Most of the time Jake acted as if he didn't want anything to do with her. Now, he wanted to know about her love life? His interest intrigued her and also gave her hope. Because if he cared...

"Why does it matter if I was involved with Mark?"

Gold sparks flashed in his eyes. "So you were."

"I didn't say that. I want to know why you care."

"Because what you do affects our son. I want to know if this man was in and out of your apartment as if it was his, if he stayed overnight—"

"All right!" she broke in, deciding answering him was the lesser of all evils. "Mark and I were never lovers. After Christopher was born, he helped me out a lot. We even dated for a while. But we both knew we were meant to be friends."

"Just friends."

She'd said it once, she wasn't going to say it again.

But Jake kept probing. "Does he know about us?"

All she could do was be honest with Jake and hope he'd eventually believe her. "Yes. He knows Christopher is yours. I didn't see him when I went back to pack up so I didn't have a chance to tell him I'd told you about Christopher."

"Why did he call?"

Sara knew Jake was showing too much interest to merely be concerned about what had happened in Wasco.

She almost smiled. Almost. "He wanted to know if Christopher would like a fire engine for Christmas."

Jake was exasperated with himself for caring who Mark was, how close he'd been to Sara, and what he meant to her now. He didn't like the idea of another man buying his son gifts, of another man helping Sara after the birth of his son. Yet guilt stabbed him, too. As Christopher's father, he should be thinking about what his son wanted for Christmas, how to make their first Christmas together special.

He tried to put the topic of Sara's romantic past aside. "Have you bought Christopher anything yet?"

She shook her head. "No. I've got to get organized."

"Maybe you and I could go Christmas shopping some night. After the auction."

Sara gave him a radiant smile that could light up all of L.A. "I'd like that."

When she smiled like that, he remembered all the good times. He hadn't looked forward to Christmas in a very long time. A child always made Christmas special. A child and...a family. He wanted his son to feel the stable solidity of a family. Jake moved away from the furniture and closer to Sara. "I'd like to make Christmas special this year for Christopher."

"So would I."

The pulse at Sara's throat fluttered, and he could count each beat. The round neckline of her T-shirt just gave him a brief glimpse of the soft skin above her breasts. He remembered the softness, the suppleness, the heat when he'd aroused her.

"I'd better finish upstairs," she murmured.

On impulse, Jake laid his hand on her arm. "Come with me to the garage. See if everything is set up the way you want it."

She studied his hand on her arm, then lifted her gaze to his. "All right." As he took his hand away, she looked around the empty room. "This is so hard."

"You can cancel the auction."

"And do what? Put it all in storage? No. I have to let go. I have Mom's china and her perfume bottle collection. The rest..." Sara shrugged. "It's not going to help me remember her better."

Jake wasn't so sure of that. Sara was putting up a brave front, but getting rid of her mother's things hurt her. He wished he could make it easier somehow. He knew how loss hurt, how it lasted. He didn't want her to regret not keeping those things that were dear to her mother.

In the garage, Sara examined each piece of furniture sitting around the perimeter. "I'm giving Mom's sideboard buffet to Aunt El. She was with her when she bought it."

As Sara talked, she slowly crossed to an old-fashioned cherry vanity. The bench was covered in needlepoint. Sitting on it, she lovingly ran her fingers over the carved handles of the small vanity drawers. "I remember sitting and watching Mom while she put on her perfume and jewelry. When I played dress-up, she'd sit me on the bench and help me apply lipstick. Then she'd say, 'You can only keep it on for a little while. Remember you're only pretending to be grown-up. You shouldn't wear lipstick until you're sixteen.'"

Jake saw the tears glisten in Sara's eyes. "Why don't you keep the vanity?"

Raising her head, Sara met his gaze in the mirror. "Where would I put it?"

"I can keep it for you. In my guest room. When you get settled somewhere, you'll have it." Though the idea of her settling somewhere other than with him was disconcerting. It shouldn't be. She'd left him. She'd lied to him. He didn't trust her. Still the idea of her and Christopher being someplace else, maybe moving someplace else, increased the ache in his heart.

Sara's bottom lip quivered, and he could tell she was fighting tears. Finally, she managed, "I would like to keep this."

He said brusquely, "Consider it done. I'll ask Nathan if I can borrow his SUV tonight."

Rising from the bench, Sara came toward him. He wasn't sure what she was going to do until she did it. Standing on tiptoe, she kissed him gently on the cheek. It was as light as the whisper of an angel—the softness of her lips, the slight brush of her breast against his arm, the sweet smell of her—and it was over faster than he could blink. But he felt all of it in every fiber of his being.

"Thank you, Jake. Your help and understanding mean a lot to me."

The urge to draw her into his arms was so strong he could imagine tasting her. But there was still too much between them—too many doubts, too much history.

He ignored the sting of desire and let her lean away. He thought again about asking her to marry him. Then he swore to himself that this time he was going to be careful because he wouldn't let her steal his heart again.

Chapter Three

The following evening, Eloise answered Jake's knock. "Jake. Sara's not here. Was she expecting you?"

"No. I thought I'd drop by and take her and Christopher for ice cream." He also wanted to tell her that he'd set up an expense fund for Christopher. Getting to know his son had been his main preoccupation during the last few weeks. But yesterday after the auction, he'd realized the proceeds from it wouldn't last Sara very long.

"You can come in if you'd like. She had a few errands."

"Christopher went with her?"

"Those two are inseparable. I guess it's because...hmm, well...it doesn't matter. Anyway, they shouldn't be too much longer. It's soon Christopher's bedtime."

"You don't mind if I wait? I have a few things I'd like to discuss with Sara."

"Of course, I don't mind. I like the company. I'm going to miss those two when they move out. But I know Sara. As soon as she finds a job, she'll find a place of their own."

A place of their own. The two of them are inseparable. Jake's heart ached, the same ache he'd felt since he'd seen Sara again, since she'd told him they had a son, since he'd become attached to his son. He hated not being able to see Christopher any time day or night. He hated feeling like the third wheel.

"I'm watching an old movie," Eloise explained. "Care to join me? Or would you rather play gin rummy?"

Jake smiled. "Think you can beat me?"

"Any day." She motioned toward the kitchen table. "Pull up a chair and we'll see who really knows how to play."

At first, time passed quickly as Eloise rejoiced in her luck, calling it skill. She won the first game. And the second... Because Jake was getting restless. Glancing at the clock became more important than the cards in his hand.

Finally, after Eloise won another round, he snapped his cards on the table. "Where did you say Sara went?"

"I think she said she might start Christmas shopping."

Was she going to do that without him? She'd said they could shop for Christopher together. With their son along, she couldn't be buying much.

At nine-thirty, Jake went to the front door and looked out. Black. Everything was black. He didn't like the feeling in his gut.

Eloise came up behind him.

"Does she usually stay out this late?"

Eloise shook her head. "No. She's particular about Christopher's bedtime. And she usually calls. But she's been having some problems with her cell phone keeping its charge. It might have died again."

"She seemed to get through the auction okay yesterday. Was she more upset than she let on?"

"I don't think so. Oh, there were some tears because she misses Jennie and yesterday was difficult, but she talked to many of the people who bought her mother's things. She told me afterward she felt they were the type to cherish them."

"She wouldn't have gone back to Wasco."

"Not without telling me."

He wasn't so sure of that. With Mark there, and if she was upset, looking for comfort.... "Do you have Mark what's-his-name's number?"

"Jake, what are you thinking?"

"I don't know what to think. I'm going to look for her."

"That would be like looking for a needle in a haystack."

"My son is out there somewhere!"

Eloise patted Jake's shoulder. "And probably perfectly safe. Do you think Sara would take any chances?"

"Eloise, I know what the streets are like. All of them. No where is safe. Damn! I'm going to call Gillian."

If Eloise wondered why, she didn't ask.

But Gillian and Nathan weren't answering their phones. They sometimes turned them off for a little peace and quiet. After all, they still acted like newlyweds. Jake left message for both of them. Then he paced.

Finally, at ten-thirty, he heard a car pull into the driveway. Jake flung open the door and ran out. Sara opened her door and looked up, obviously surprised to see him.

He gulped in a deep breath. Christopher was safe. He could see him sleeping in his car seat. Sara was safe. *So don't fly off the handle.* Right. As if he hadn't been sweating buckets since nine o'clock.

"Do you need help?" he asked Sara gruffly.

"Christopher's asleep. If you could carry him to the bedroom, I'll get the packages."

Packages. She was worried about the damn packages. "Are you all right?" His gaze appraised her, noting her clothes weren't mussed or torn.

"I'm fine. We had a flat tire. I thought I could fix it myself but the lugs were too tight. By the time the auto club arrived, it was nine-thirty. My cell phone died again and... She must have seen something in his expression because she said, "I didn't mean to worry anyone."

Worry. More like panic and fear. He hated the way they made him feel helpless and out of control.

Jake carried Christopher to the bedroom and couldn't sit still long enough to help Sara undress their son or tuck him in. He needed air. Lots of it.

As Sara removed Christopher's shoes, Jake said, "I'll be on the front porch. Come out when you're finished."

Sara's wide blue eyes held hundreds of questions. He didn't have the answers. Standing on the porch, looking out into the black, knowing the terrors that lurked out there, he suddenly had one answer. The most important one.

He hadn't wanted another child. But now he was a father again. That was the reality. So how could he best safeguard Christopher and prepare him for life?

By giving him a stable home and two parents who would put their son first. He and Sara could do that most effectively under the same roof. How stable could Christopher's life be if they were constantly trying to coordinate two households, two schedules, two sets of rules? He and Sara needed to parent together.

If they got married, Sara could forget about finding a job, stay home, and be a full-time mother. And he would have constant access to his son—not part time fathering.

A marriage for Christopher's sake made perfect sense. Now all he had to do was persuade Sara. After all, why shouldn't she agree? She wouldn't have to worry about finances or the future. In fact, maybe this was why she'd returned—because raising a son was too difficult to handle on her own. If that was the case, she might jump at the offer of marriage.

The minutes passed like years as Jake waited. When Sara stepped onto the porch, a sweater thrown over her shoulders, his heart pounded.

"Jake, Aunt El said you were really worried. If I could have called, I would have."

"I understand." He looked up at the sky, devoid of stars. "Marry me, Sara."

Sara's heart raced so fast she could hardly breathe. This proposal of Jake's, if that's what it was, was nothing like his first proposal four years ago. That one had been romantic and gentle, a question amid yellow roses and candlelight. Now, he was standing in the black of night and his proposal was anything but romantic.

Yet maybe he still had feelings for her. Maybe the love hadn't died. "Why do you want to get married?" she asked softly, almost afraid to hear his reply.

He didn't hesitate, and his expression said the answer

should be obvious. "To give Christopher a stable life—two parents, a home where he feels safe and secure."

"And what about us?" She held her breath.

"Us?" He looked again up to the sky, and then with a frown he faced her. "I don't know about us."

As close as they were, she could smell the familiar scent of the soap Jake used. Its clean, masculine aroma was as recognizable to her as the sound of his voice. Did he want to marry her only because of Christopher? Or did he still have feelings for her? Would he want her to share his bed?

"Do you intend...I mean—" She didn't know a subtle way to ask if he wanted to make love with her.

"Just because we're living together doesn't mean we have to sleep together," he said quietly.

He must be a lot stronger than she was or else she'd hurt him so badly when she'd called off the wedding that he no longer desired her. Jake was a sensual man. To marry her and remain celibate seemed unlikely. "If we're married, what do you expect?"

The intensity of his stance and expression didn't change. "I expect you to make a home for us and be faithful to our marriage, just as I will."

"But if we're not sleeping together—"

"Celibacy is nothing new to me. I haven't been a monk, but in this day and age I've been damn careful. I hope you have, too."

"The right person never came along...a man I'd want to be intimate with."

Jake's stare bored into her even in the shadows. "Are you saying I'm the first and only man you've ever been with?"

"Yes."

His gaze skimmed over her from her hair to her toes. "I wish I could believe you."

"I wouldn't lie to you, Jake."

He turned away from her, toward the house next door. "But you did. You didn't tell me the real reason for calling off the wedding, and you didn't tell me I had a son. Once trust is broken, Sara, it's real hard to fix."

She almost felt as if he couldn't stand to look at her, and that hurt so bad. "I wish you could understand."

Facing her again, he admitted, "I can't. All I know is that nothing on this earth will keep me away from Christopher. I want legal rights to him and marrying you will give me those. As for the rest, we'll take one day at a time."

She realized now when she'd canceled their wedding, she'd hurt Jake irrevocably. He'd trusted her with his past and his future and now he felt as if she'd betrayed that trust. She'd never meant to. She'd thought she'd loved him enough to do what was best for him. But she knew now she'd been wrong not to tell him about her pregnancy, not to tell him about Christopher.

She'd always respected Jake's sense of right and wrong, the code of ethics he followed. She'd trust him with her life and their son's. She remembered their Friday nights, the yellow rose that had symbolized their growing relationship, the bond that had developed from the first moment they'd talked. Jake was a strong man and sometimes too stoic and silent. But when he let his guard down, when he cared about someone, no man could be more compassionate or caring.

One evening, soon after they'd started dating, Jennie Standish had dropped her wedding band down the drain. It had slipped off as she'd rinsed dishes. Jake hadn't hesitated to roll up his sleeves and work for two hours until he found the ring trapped in a section of pipe under the sink. He'd realized what that wedding band had meant to her mother.

When Sara had backed out of their wedding, thinking she was giving Jake what he wanted, she'd felt as if her heart had been torn from her. Loving him, marrying him now, could make her feel whole again.

Did he still love her? Could she accept his proposal if he was only offering it because of Christopher?

Yes, because she still loved him. One day at a time with Jake would be better than one day at a time without him. Eventually, he'd trust her again. She'd see to that. Eventually he'd realize how much she loved him and then, maybe he'd feel love again, too. And together they would parent their son. If she hadn't been so young, if she hadn't been so afraid marriage to Jake and a child he hadn't wanted would kill their love, she'd have married him four years ago. But the past was past. All she could do was make up for it the best she could.

"Yes, Jake. I'll marry you. On one condition."

His voice was wary. "What?"

"Any decision about Christopher's well-being we make together. No unilateral decisions—on anything." She knew how strong-minded Jake could be. She wasn't about to let him take away any of her rights as a mother.

He studied her for what seemed like hours. "Done." Extending his hand, he waited for her to take it.

As she placed her hand in his, she was aware of the largeness of his, the firmness of his, the strength that was so much a part of him—that had led him to see the straight and narrow since he was a child. Jake might not trust her, but she trusted him.

He shook her hand quickly, then let go. But for that transient moment, she felt connected to him again, and that connection gave her hope.

A week later, Eloise zipped up the back of Sara's dress and smiled at her in the dresser's mirror. The dress was the palest pink lace, gently and femininely form-fitting. She wore her mother's strand of pearls.

When her aunt handed her the bouquet of white roses and baby's breath, Sara looked like a bride.

The problem was she didn't feel like a bride. "Aunt El, am I doing the right thing?"

Her aunt, dressed in mauve chiffon, straightened her sash. "You've loved Jake for a long time."

"But I'm afraid he doesn't love me anymore. He loves Christopher. He's patient and gentle, and it's so hard to believe he didn't want to be a father again. But at times he tries not to even look at me. I see the pain when he does, and sometimes even with Christopher. What kind of life are we going to have if he's only marrying me because of our son?"

"Child, there's still time to call this off. Is that what you want to do?"

Sara ran through all of it in her mind again as she

had so many times since she'd shaken Jake's hand, since she'd felt her love for Jake grow each time she saw him with their son, since she'd seen a doctor and asked for birth control pills. If she called off the wedding, she would lose Jake. She knew that as well as she knew her name. She just wished she had a guarantee that time would heal because today her worst fear was that he was marrying her only for Christopher's sake, not because he still loved her. Could that be a basis for a marriage?

Yes, it could. For this marriage. She had to believe Jake would come to love her again. Did she want to call off the ceremony? No.

Shaking her head so vigorously that her pearl earrings swung, she said, "I don't want to call it off. I want to marry Jake."

"Then square your shoulders, hold your head high, and walk over to those stairs like the lady I know you are."

Sara hugged her aunt. "I'm glad you're here. I just wish Mom could be here, too."

As Eloise leaned back, she said, "Your mother's here, Sara. Guiding you a little differently from when she was alive, but guiding you just the same."

Sara kissed her aunt's cheek. "Thank you."

Eloise gave her a tight squeeze as they heard music begin. Sara knew it was a CD, but she didn't care. This was her wedding day, and she'd make the most of it.

Jake stood in the living room beside Nathan Bradley, his best man. Christopher, who held a white satin pillow, rocked from one foot to the other at the foot of the stairs, waiting for his mother. Two gold bands lay on the top of the pillow. When Jake had asked Sara about the type of ring she preferred, the band was what she'd picked. She could have had anything she wanted. He'd pointed out several that were channel-set with diamonds. But she'd shaken her head and asked if he'd wear one, too. Why not? After all, they were getting married.

Beside him, Nathan asked in a low voice so the minister a few feet away couldn't hear, "Are you having second thoughts?"

"No."

"You don't have to marry her to get legal rights to Christopher."

"I know." Nathan wasn't only Gillian's husband, but a good friend. He was informed about custody law because of his own situation with his two daughters from a previous marriage.

His friend kept his voice low. "I want you to make sure you know what you're doing."

Getting married. Jake supposed it meant faith in the future to most people. He'd thought it had meant that to Mary Beth. Then she'd walked out when they could have pulled together. Not that he blamed her. She couldn't forgive him for Davie's death, and she certainly couldn't forget it.

Jake had wanted to start fresh when he'd met Sara, maybe so he could begin to forget himself. Sara had given him the chance to do that...for a few months. Then she'd broken her promise to marry him. She'd left when, in a sense, he'd needed her most. He wouldn't need her, or any woman, again. He'd concentrate on Christopher despite the pain, maybe because of it, and he'd take care of Sara because she was his son's mother.

"I know what I'm doing," Jake responded in a decisive tone that he realized wouldn't reassure Nathan. But reassuring his best man was low on his priority list.

"Jake, a child isn't enough to hold a marriage together. You can be a good parent without marrying Sara Standish."

Taking his gaze from his son, Jake faced Nathan. "I want to be a full time father. I've seen what happens to kids whose parents are split. Remember, I spend most Sundays at the community center. I work with kids who are looking for approval wherever they can get it even if it means belonging to a gang. I want better for my son. I want better than I had. I want to keep him safe."

"My girls are doing just fine."

Jake didn't mean to insult Nathan or insinuate he was doing something wrong. "Your situation is the exception, and you know it. Just stand up for me, Nathan. I don't need your advice."

"That's a matter of opinion," Nathan muttered.

Long ago, Jake had learned he couldn't please everyone, not even people he cared about. He could only do what he thought was right. That's the way he'd lived his life. Being a cop had reduced his vision to black and white. Shades of gray could have gotten him killed. Giving the benefit of the doubt, feeling pity for someone, had brought down more than one good man. Even as a private investigator the fact had been driven home again and again—there was truth and there were lies. Husbands cheated on wives, wives cheated on husbands, con artists scammed women, white collar thieves tried to take advantage of the system. Truth usually found the lie. But right didn't always win over wrong. He thought about Davie and felt the familiar pain.

He glanced around the room, looking for a distraction. Gillian smiled at him. What Jake liked about his investigative work with Gillian was the sincerity of it, the truth of it, and the rightness of it. They helped people find other people. Many clients they'd helped had given generously for the work they did, and Jake had set up a foundation to fund their work. Those who could pay did. Those who couldn't were helped anyway.

As the music swelled, Jake turned his attention again to the stairs. Eloise came down the steps first. Christopher grinned and waved at her. His pillow tilted and Jake was glad Eloise had pinned the rings.

Then Sara appeared on the steps, and Jake felt as if someone had smacked him in the solar plexus with a fist. She was a vision—lace, softness, innocence. What kind of marriage could they have when he felt such mixed feelings about her?

For the past four years, he'd thought about her— when his defenses were down, in the dead of night, when he came home to an empty house after a business trip. He'd thought about their months together, that one night....

Sara had been a virgin when they'd made love so he'd never had a doubt Christopher was his son. Christopher's birth date coincided with that night exactly. What Jake didn't understand was how Sara could have thrown away what they'd shared...how she could have run out on him...how she could have kept his son from him for so long.

Even though their courtship had been a whirlwind of emotions and passion, he'd thought he'd known Sara, despite their views of the world—hers slightly naive because of her age, his more cynical because of his age. At the time, the ten year age difference hadn't mattered. He'd fallen in love with Sara because of her fresh enthusiasm, her optimism. But now he realized he hadn't known her at all.

He was marrying a stranger.

His bride paused at the bottom step and took her son's hand, her smile saying she was not at all perturbed Christopher hadn't stayed in his spot beside Jake. Sara's smile did as much to arouse Jake as her curves subtly outlined by the lace. When she faced him, her smile faded.

Jake turned toward the minister, ready to listen to the words that would change his life.

The ceremony took mere minutes. A greeting. Vows. The exchange of rings. Sara's eyes glistened, and again Jake wondered who she was, what the future would bring. He wasn't thinking beyond a life with his son, beyond the chance to nurture and safeguard this little boy in a way he hadn't been able to nurture and protect Davie.

At the end of the ceremony, the silver-haired minister said, "You may now kiss the bride."

Jake looked down into Sara's sky blue eyes. Eloise, Nathan, Christopher and Gillian—who was cuddling her baby—waited expectantly. Sara's perfume wafted around him. Her soft skin beckoned him. Her dress asked for his touch. He pressed his hand against the small of her back as he bent his head. The brush of his lips on Sara's was fleeting, a heartbeat, but enough to shake the foundation of his control.

Straightening quickly, he stepped away. He would not give in to desire that could lead to heartache. He would not show Sara he was vulnerable where she was concerned. He would not give up his heart another time.

Eloise hugged Sara and kissed her as the minister shook Jake's hand. After Nathan and Gillian congratulated the couple, Eloise announced, "Refreshments are in the dining room. Help yourselves to punch while the bride and groom cut the cake."

Standing close by his side, Sara murmured to Jake, "If you don't want to do this, we don't have to."

"Your aunt went to a lot of trouble. Let's not disappoint her." He crossed to the dining room and the cake on the table, waiting for Sara to join him.

After he handed her the knife, he covered her hand with his as they cut through the layers. When he withdrew his hand, Sara managed to shift the slice to a white paper plate. She broke off a piece and held it between her thumb and forefinger, then offered him the rest. He, too, broke off a piece.

As Sara's fingers came closer to Jake's lips, he fed her. She opened her mouth, and he placed the cake inside. Her lips touched his fingers, and he felt the velvet softness of her tongue. His breath hitched, but he didn't have time to do anything but open his mouth. Somehow her finger got caught between his lips.

She pulled away, but not before he vividly remembered tasting her lips and her neck and...

Sara's world reeled. The taste of cake, icing and Jake was enough to make her dizzy. The man beside her was her husband, but he didn't seem happy about it. The past week he'd been remote, and today was no different. Jake had always been an introvert, but now he seemed even more distant—at least with her. With Nathan and Gillian and even with her aunt, he didn't appear to have a problem making conversation. And certainly not with his son. But with her...

She and Jake both took a step back as if the cake and the meaning behind it were too incendiary to accept. She saw Nathan Bradley exchange a look with his wife, and she wondered what Jake had told the couple about this marriage.

Christopher sidled up beside Sara. "Cake, Mommy?"

As it had for the past four years, Sara's focus shifted to her son. She tweaked his nose, grateful for the surge of love that always filled her when she looked at him.

The reception didn't last long. Without Eloise's conversational maneuvers and Christopher's chattering, the hour or so would have been even more awkward. The minister left first, then Nathan and Gillian. Jake tugged open his tie, unbuttoned his charcoal suit coat and shrugged it off. He tossed it over a chair and rolled up his shirt sleeves. "Where are your suitcases?"

Sara touched the pearls at her neck. "Wait until I change and I'll help you."

His gaze slid over her. "That's not necessary." He crooked his finger at Christopher who came running, the white jacket that matched his pants flapping as he ran. "How would you like to get out of these clothes and get comfortable before we go home?"

Sara crouched down beside her son. "Remember I told you we're going to move in with your daddy?"

Christopher nodded then stuck one finger in his mouth and talked around it. "An' I c'n bring Teddy?"

Jake also bent down to his son's level. "You sure can. And your cars and everything else, too. My house will be your new home."

Christopher looked up at Sara. "We're gonna live with Daddy and see Aunt El—but not Nana. Nana's in heaven."

After an awkward moment, Jake said, "Yes, she is." He clasped his son's shoulder. "Would you like to go pick out a swing for my backyard?"

The three-year-old took his finger from his mouth and broke into a grin. "Yeah!"

Jake smiled, adding, "And when we do get to my house, there's a surprise for you."

"What?"

With a wink, he ruffled his son's hair. "You'll just have to wait and see."

"Soon?"

"As soon as you change clothes and we pick out a swing."

Christopher grabbed Sara's hand. "C'mon, Mommy. Change."

"I have to clean up..."

Eloise had overheard the conversation. "I'll take care of the cups and crumbs. Go on. The sooner you change, the sooner you can begin your new life."

Sara looked down at her son who couldn't wait for his surprise. If only starting a new life were that easy.

Not only did they shop for a swing set, but Jake let Christopher pick out a sliding board and jungle gym, too. While their son tried out the swing that was set up in the store's parking lot, Sara nudged Jake's elbow. "Try not to go overboard." His shoulders stiffened and his jaw set. She realized she should have been more tactful. "I just mean—"

"Sara, I will buy my son anything I damn well please."

Patiently, she returned, "A swing set and jungle gym won't make your house into a home."

"A swing set, jungle gym and anything else Christopher might enjoy will help him feel comfortable. Just because you might not have been able to give him everything you wanted, doesn't mean I can't."

"Jake, we have an agreement."

"Yes, we do. I did not make a unilateral decision. You're here with me."

"But you're not listening."

"I heard you. You want me to not buy Christopher a jungle gym because it will make you feel better in some way. Tell me why he shouldn't have it."

"I don't want you to spoil him. I don't want you to think buying him presents will make you a father!" As soon as she said it, she regretted it.

Jake's voice was as cold as the end-of-October day was warm. "I expect I can read some books on the subject since my practical experience is lacking. We both know why it's lacking, so maybe you should take that into consideration when I want to buy my son something."

There was nothing Sara could say to that, nothing to defend her position. She couldn't prevent Jake from wanting to make up for the years he'd missed. Jake didn't wait for a response from her as he strode toward his son, waited for him to jump off the swing and climb onto the glider also attached to the cross bar.

Sara watched them together—father and son—and wished she had never run away, wished she had faced Jake with the truth before Christopher was born. Jake's resentment then couldn't have been any worse than his anger was now.

A short time later, despite whether Jake wanted her help or not, Sara carried the last of her belongings into the house. She had brought her car over yesterday, and Jake had driven her and Christopher to Eloise's last evening.

Jake took her suitcase and garment bag to the guest room at the end of the hall. Christopher followed on his daddy's heels, lugging a small carry-all with his miniature cars.

After Sara set her cosmetics case on the dresser, she hung her wedding dress in the closet.

Jake beckoned to Christopher. "C'mon, sport. I'll show you your surprise."

Christopher ran down the hall after Jake. Sara heard, "Look, Mommy. Come look!"

As curious as her son, she quickly followed him and stood in the doorway of the second guest bedroom, surveying the interior which had changed drastically since she'd seen it last. "When did you do this?"

"The furniture came this morning."

A youth bed with a bookcase headboard stood against one wall. A table with four chairs, Christopher's size, was placed beside a chalkboard and toy box in the shape of a football. A toy bulldozer and steamroller decorated the shelves where a variety of books also waited.

Christopher opened the toy box. "Wow! Cars and..." He lifted out a red stuffed toy. "Elmo!"

Jake's lean face showed obvious joy over Christopher's pleasure. His gaze connected with Sara's. She walked over to the bed. "Think you'll like sleeping here?"

"You'll be over there?" He pointed to the room where Jake had deposited the suitcases.

"Yes, I will. And your Daddy will be right across the hall. I brought your night light, too. We'll plug it in before you go to bed."

Christopher sat on the bed and bounced a few times, obviously happy with his room.

Sara smiled and Jake smiled back. The simple exchange made her feel better about the wedding that didn't seem like a wedding, about the separate rooms, about their past.

Jake asked Sara, "Where would you like to go for supper?"

"That's up to you," she deferred, still feeling her way, not knowing what Jake had in mind.

"There's a nice restaurant a few miles from here. Quiet, stained glass windows. The service is good. I don't think it would be too long for Christopher to sit. Or if you'd like, we can order and I'll go get it."

"I'd like to go out. Especially since it's our wedding day," she said quietly.

Jake's brown eyes darkened.

"Do I need to change?"

His jaw tensed as he surveyed her royal blue blouse and slacks. "You're fine the way you are. I'll change and we can go."

Sara had always felt as if Jake could see right through her. Since she knew he knew what was underneath the clothes, she couldn't prevent the heat flushing her cheeks.

Jake didn't comment but went into his bedroom, a room she'd shared with him one night long ago.

Christopher's day had been a long, exciting one. His eyelids started to droop by dessert, and he fell asleep in the car on the way home. Jake carried Christopher up to his new bedroom. Sara undressed the little boy while Jake found a pair of pajamas in the suitcase.

"Sleepy, Mommy," Christopher grumbled.

"I know, honey. Let's go to the bathroom and then you can crawl right into bed."

Jake helped Sara put Christopher into his pajamas. He held a sleeve as Sara guided the little boy's hand through. While she buttoned up the shirt, he plugged the night light into the receptacle by the window.

Sara found Christopher's teddy bear at the foot of the bed and tucked the toy in beside the little boy. Then she leaned close and kissed his cheek. "Good night, little one. Happy dreams."

Sara saw Jake look down at his son and brush his fine hair across his brow before following her into the hall and down the stairs. She wasn't sure what to do next.

Conversation seemed preferable to the awkward silence.

There was something she knew she had to say. "Thank you for Christopher's room."

His brows arched as if her thank you surprised him. "You're welcome. You really think he likes it?"

"I know he does. Especially the toy box. It was thoughtful of you."

"Not excessive?"

She shook her head. "No. Jake, I'm sorry about what I said..."

Bracing his hand on the wall above her head, he admitted, "I thought about what you said, and you're right. Buying Christopher presents won't make me a father. I have a feeling it's going to be trial and error."

She smiled and her heart raced at Jake's closeness. She could still smell the scent of his soap mixed with his own male scent that made her stomach quiver. "Aren't most things?"

"I suppose." He straightened and towered over her. "I have some work to do that I put aside this week. I'll be in my office if you need anything."

"Oh." She couldn't hide her disappointment.

He heard it. "What?"

She shrugged. "I thought maybe we could talk for a while."

His brows arched. "About?"

"Anything. Jake, this is our wedding day."

"And I'm doing the best I can with it. What do you want? Champagne and toasting each other by candlelight?"

"A toast to our future would be nice."

He ran his hand quickly over his face. "Sara, I'm still so angry about what you did—"

Before she thought better of it, she clasped his arm. "You didn't want children. Can't you understand I thought I was making the best decision for both of us?"

He glanced down at her hand and she took it away, but not before she felt the muscle, the springy hair, the pure maleness of him.

"Why now, Sara? Why after all this time did you decide to tell me? Because you can't make it on your own?"

"No! I'm sure I can find another job, especially here. And Christopher and I have always had what we needed. I came back for lots of reasons. Over the years I've missed Dad terribly. He died at such an important time in my life—right before I started high school, when I was beginning to look at boys differently, when I had so many doubts about myself, what I wanted to do with my life. The last three years, parenting Christopher alone, I realized how difficult those years must have been for Mom. Especially when I lost her so suddenly, I realized Christopher needed more than me, more than visiting Aunt El now and then. He needed a connection with his father if that was possible."

"You really thought I might not want that connection?"

"I honestly didn't know."

Jake looked down at her, searching her face, his gaze lingering on her lips. "You didn't know me."

"Maybe not," she whispered.

"And I never knew you. I never suspected you could hide something so important."

His brown eyes held disappointment and sadness, too much for him to disguise. When she'd walked out on him, had she killed his love for her? She bit her lip. "I'm sorry."

He shook his head. "Sorry isn't good enough. It won't make up for the years I've lost."

"What can I do?"

"That's just it, Sara. There's nothing you can do. Maybe time will help. I don't know."

She struggled to hide the emotions coursing through her, but especially the way she still felt about Jake—although he obviously had lost all feeling for her, except his anger and resentment. "And you think we can still have a marriage?"

He jammed his hands into the pockets of his black shorts. "We can be parents to Christopher."

"Don't we matter?"

"Not right now."

Fighting back tears, she made one last attempt at some kind of relationship. "At least let me be your friend."

"I trust my friends, Sara."

What he didn't say was clear. He didn't trust her. She swallowed hard, trying to ignore how much his words hurt, trying to look at their life together realistically. "I usually make breakfast around eight. Is that all right?"

He studied her for a moment. "Eight is fine. I usually just grab a cup of coffee but that might change with Christopher around. I went to the store yesterday and stocked up on everything I could think of. If you can't find something, just ask."

Her gaze met his. "I will."

Familiar gold sparks flashed in his eyes. He reached

out and brushed a stray lock of hair away from her cheek. "You looked beautiful today, Sara."

She had no answer, no murmured "thank you," because all her emotions jammed as the heat of his fingers scorched her cheek, as remembered tenderness was evident in his touch.

Dropping his hand, he said, "I'll see you in the morning."

All she could do was nod, watch him walk away, and wonder if marrying him was an even bigger mistake than running away when she was twenty.

Chapter Four

"Mommy! Mommee—"

Sara came awake and was on her feet instantly. Without bothering to grab her robe, she dashed toward her son's cry, sliding onto the bed beside him and holding him in her arms. "What's wrong, honey?"

The hall light went on and Jake's shadow fell across the bed. He waited there, watching Sara, watching his son.

Christopher tightened his arms around Sara's neck. "I wanna sleep wif you."

Sara hugged him then leaned away. "Okay. But can you tell me why?"

"'Cause...I don' know. I just wanna sleep wif you."

"Did you have a bad dream?"

He shrugged.

"Are you afraid to sleep in here by yourself?"

He nodded.

"You have Teddy with you," she soothed.

"I wanna go wif you."

Sara combed his hair back from his forehead. "You can sleep with me if you're sure that's what you want to do. Or I could stay here with you until you fall asleep again."

Christopher poked his finger in his mouth and thought about it. "Okay. Can I sleep wif Elmo, too?"

Jake strode across the room, plucked the plush toy from the shelf and set it in Christopher's lap. His hand brushed Sara's midriff. Suddenly she was aware of the intimacy of the situation. At first, her only concern had been Christopher. Now, sitting before Jake, his bare chest sprinkled with a matt of curling hair, his black silk shorts riding low on his hips, she was more aware than ever that this was their wedding night, and they were spending it in separate rooms.

She tried to speak but had to clear her throat and try again. "We'll be all right if you want to go back to bed."

His gaze flicked over her quickly, then he slowly crossed to the doorway. "Christopher, would you like me to leave the hall light on?"

The three-year-old nodded.

Jake gave his son a smile. "I'll see you in the morning."

Sara waited until Jake was back in his room before she slid down into Christopher's bed and he squiggled and snuggled with Elmo and Teddy, finally settling against her. "'Night, Mommy," he murmured.

She kissed his cheek.

Sara had not intended to fall asleep. She'd planned to wait until Christopher slept before slipping back to her room. But when she opened her eyes and saw the clock on her son's shelf read four a.m., she realized she'd dozed off.

Christopher lay on his side, Elmo under his arm, his bear by his side. Sara sat up and swung her legs soundlessly over the side. Stopping in the doorway, she made sure her son was still sleeping.

She'd turned toward her room when Jake appeared in the hall. Startled, she jumped.

"I didn't mean to scare you."

"You didn't. I just didn't expect you to still be awake."

"I heard you get out of Christopher's bed."

"I didn't make any noise."

"Squeaky floor board," Jake explained. "In the dead of night, instincts take over and I can't forget I was a cop."

His brown eyes held her where she stood, though she knew she should get back to her room. His face was too close to hers, his voice was too night-husky. He was danger and safety and too much man for her peace of mind as he stood within reach. Her pulse fluttered at her throat, and her nipples hardened.

Jake's gaze brushed across her lips and lingered on the neckline of her peach cotton gown. Her common sense told her to run. Her heart told her to stay. If she could make him want her again...

"Do you always give him a choice?"

"What?" Her voice came out as a whisper.

"Christopher. I thought for sure he'd want to sleep in your room, but you gave him the choice."

"He's getting more independent. If he makes the decision, he's usually satisfied with it. Fewer tantrums and problems in the long run."

Jake's brows arched. "I can't imagine him having tantrums."

She couldn't help but smile. "You might be in for a surprise. He can be quite stubborn when he wants his own way."

"I guess I've been a playmate more than a parent. I'll try to be more aware of that. I do remember Davie at that age—" He stopped abruptly. "I've watched how you talk with Christopher, how you handle him. You're a good mother, Sara."

"My mom taught me everything I know. She was the best role model I could have ever had."

"You miss her."

Sara could feel quick hot tears that she willed away. "I miss her a lot."

The nerve in Jake's jaw worked as, again, he ran his eyes over her from head to toe. When his gaze reached her bare feet, he said, "You'd better get back to bed."

She nodded but couldn't seem to move away.

He did. At his bedroom door, he paused. "Should I leave the hall light on?"

"In case he wakes up again."

Jake looked toward his son's bedroom. "I'll see you in the morning."

Jake heard Sara walk back to her room. He sank down onto his king-size bed and ran both hands through his hair. Her footsteps were so light, like an angel barely touching the earth. In that simple gown... He held out his hand. It was trembling, and he felt like a fool. Seeing her sleep-mussed hair, her pink cheeks, their son in her arms—

Damn!

Dropping his hand to his knee, he remembered the way her breasts responded to his nearness. Sara Standish Donovan was not an angel. This time he wouldn't let her get close enough to see his heart, his soul, or his desire. He'd always been good at keeping people at bay. He'd had years of practice. First with his father. Bud Donovan had been a mean drunk. Jake had learned early to stay away and show no emotion. And with his mother...

She'd become a broken woman by the time his father left. The doctors had said she'd died of an overdose of sleeping pills. Jake knew better. She'd died of a shattered heart.

No, he wouldn't let Sara get close enough to do any damage. All he had to do was keep up his guard. He'd care for and protect his son and treat Sara like a room-mate. How hard could that be?

Sara started breakfast the next morning, agonizing over her conversation with Jake the night before, their en-counters in Christopher's room and the hall. Their wedding night.

She cracked an egg into a bowl. She felt Jake before she saw him. Shivers skipped up her back and when she looked over her shoulder, she saw the guarded look on his face. He wore cut-off denims and a black T-shirt with the letters advertising SEA WORLD almost washed off, and although remote, he looked as tired as she felt.

Her heart beat faster as he came to the counter where she was standing. She said the only thing that came to mind. "Good morning."

He lifted a mug from the wooden tree. "Morning."

"Christopher was still sleeping when I came down."

"When I looked in on him, he looked so peaceful. Made me wonder what I'd have to do to sleep that soundly."

Sara didn't know whether to pursue that line of thought. Deciding against it, she stuck to the mundane. "I'm making scrambled eggs for Christopher and me. How would you like yours?"

"Scrambled is fine." Jake poured coffee into his mug, his elbow brushing hers. His eyes collided with hers.

Her body pulsed with the desire to have him hold her in his arms. Ducking her head, she cracked another egg into the bowl. "Do you have outside appointments today?"

"Why?"

She sighed, hoping every conversation they had wouldn't be such a struggle. "I have to go to Mom's and make one last check. It shouldn't take long. I can take Christopher along or I can leave him here with you."

Jake stared into his coffee, then raised his head. "Would you like me to go along?"

"You'd do that?"

Jake took a cautious sip of the hot coffee. "We're married, Sara. If you want me there, I'll go with you."

"I'd like that. Is after lunch all right?"

"That's fine." Taking his mug with him, Jake headed for his office. "Let me know when breakfast is ready."

As Jake left the kitchen, Sara wondered if he had the rules for their marriage written down somewhere. He seemed to know them. She didn't.

The next day, Sara put Christopher down for his nap feeling as if she needed one, too. Maybe the emotional upheaval from the past month had caught up with her—her mother's death, living in L.A., telling Jake about Christopher, getting married. Yesterday, Jake had stood by her side as she walked through an empty house. She'd longed to turn to him again for comfort, but she couldn't. He was there physically but emotionally he was hundreds of miles away. She didn't know how to reach him.

At the living room, she heard voices coming from Jake's office—Gillian must have arrived while she was upstairs. Eager to get to know Jake's partner better, Sara headed toward the sun-filled room.

As she stood in the doorway, she could see Jake standing at Gillian's desk, leaning over her. His head was very near his partner's. He said something and Gillian laughed. His smile said he shared her humor. They seemed so easy together, so...friendly. Jealousy stabbed Sara and she knew there was no reason for it. Gillian and Nathan were happily married. Weren't they?

Jake laid his hand on Gillian's shoulder.

Sara didn't think she'd moved or made a sound, but Gillian turned toward her. "Hi, there. I just stopped in to catch up on cases."

Gillian's smile was pleasant, her tone friendly without

a shred of guilt. Sara's gaze went to Jake's hand on his partner's shoulder. He saw the look, waited a moment, then removed it.

Gillian stepped right into the awkwardness. "Sara, how would you like to go shopping with me sometime or maybe have dinner?"

The invitation was a surprise. There was a warmth that emanated from Jake's partner, a caring that was hard to resist. "I'd like that."

"I'll check Nathan's schedule and see when he can watch Matthew." She smiled. "He doesn't like to use a babysitter unless it's necessary."

"Where's Matthew now?" Sara asked.

"With Nathan. He took the afternoon off to spend with his girls and son." Gillian shuffled the papers in front of her into a pile and stood. "I'd better get going. We're having a barbecue this evening and I told Nathan I'd stop at the bakery for dessert." She pushed her chair back and took her purse from the desktop. On her way out, she said, "I'll get back to you about getting together."

Gillian had closed the front door when Sara commented, "She seems nice."

"She's more than nice."

Sara couldn't tell if there was simply respect in Jake's voice or more. "How long have she and Nathan been married?"

"It was three years in August."

"Did you know Gillian before she married Nathan?"

"Why all the questions, Sara?"

"I just wondered."

His eyes narrowed. "I knew Nathan first."

"Oh."

"What's on your mind?"

"Nothing really. You and Gillian seem...close."

"We're partners and we're friends."

"I see."

"But I don't. I don't think you're saying what you're thinking."

Before Sara married Jake, she'd decided she'd never keep anything from him again. Yet telling him what she'd felt when she came in and saw him and Gillian together... "I wondered what your feelings are for Gillian. You seem so comfortable with her...so affectionate."

Jake studied her for a few long moments, then responded, "From the moment I met Gillian, I realized she brought out the best in the people she's around."

He wasn't telling her anything. She was trying to be honest and open with him, but he was more closed than ever. "Did you mind when she married Nathan?"

"Nathan's a good friend."

"But did you mind?" She could be just as stubborn as he was.

His eyes became piercing brown as he stood perfectly still. "No, I didn't mind. Nathan and Gillian are made for each other. No one could interfere in their relationship even if they tried."

He still wasn't telling her his feelings. "Are you attracted to Gillian?"

His voice became as sharp as his eyes. "Dammit, Sara. Why the inquisition? I'm married to you."

"I'm not sure how much that means." Her words shot out unexpectedly, surprising her and Jake.

With restrained patience, he explained, "Gillian is a partner and a friend. I like her because she's easy to be around, she's sincere and honest and can read people better than anyone I know. But that's it. I don't want her in my bed. I don't wish she and Nathan weren't married. Does that satisfy your curiosity?"

The month had been too long, too fraught with emotion for her to spar with Jake now. "I wasn't curious. I was jealous." On that admission, she left Jake's office and went to the kitchen to start supper.

That night, Jake listened as Sara read Christopher a story. When she imitated the voices of Papa Bear, Mama Bear, and Baby Bear, Christopher giggled and said, "Do it again, Mommy." Sara smiled and repeated the section.

That smile. Jake wanted to kiss it more than he wanted to find his newest client's lost high school sweetheart. Why did Sara have the power to get to him? It was purely physical—her smell, her taste, the sight of her. She was just a woman, a woman who'd lied to him...and left him.

When Sara finished the story, she kissed Christopher good night. Jake gave his son a hug, then followed her down the stairs. The past two nights he'd gone to his office after they'd put Christopher to bed. It was safer that way. But tonight, he had to get something straight between them.

Sara sat on the sofa in the living room and picked up a book she'd been reading the evening before. Looking up at him with surprise on her face, she asked, "You're not working tonight?"

He sat on the arm of the sofa. "In a minute. I have something to tell you first."

She frowned. "Good or bad?"

"I have to go out of town."

"A case?"

"Yes. I'm leaving Sunday evening."

"Do you go out of town often?"

"It depends on our clients. Sometimes I have to follow a lead in person."

"Gillian doesn't?"

"When she has to. I...uh...should explain something about Gillian. She's got this gift for finding people. She's psychic."

Sara was silent for a good minute. "So you use your experience and connections as a cop and she does the rest."

"Sort of. You know, if I told most people what I just told you, they'd be skeptical."

Sara shrugged. "If you believe in Gillian, why should I doubt her? You don't believe without proof."

Sara was right about that. For him, seeing was believing. "I had first-hand proof. Nathan's girls were missing, and Gillian helped find them. Her gift is amazing." Sara's blue eyes clouded, and he remembered what she'd said earlier. "If it's true you're jealous, you have no reason to be...of Gillian or anyone else. I told you I'd be faithful to our marriage, and I will be."

The clouds didn't leave her eyes. "Are you sorry you married me?"

"We haven't been married long enough to have regrets," he replied cautiously.

"Our lives are so separate, except for Christopher."

"It's got to be that way, Sara. Until we can find some common ground." Until he could begin to trust her again.

Her eyes were so blue, her expression so vulnerable. He was drawn toward common ground and Sara's softness.

She tilted her head up as he lowered his. She was everything womanly. His body responded to hers as if they'd never been apart. Her lips weren't enough. He wanted to taste her secrets, find out if she was playing some game with him, remember the ecstasy they'd once shared.

When his tongue breached her lips, she opened them freely, welcoming his desire. He didn't take time to tease, but stroked against her again and again, raising the stakes, seeing how far she'd go. It wasn't that he wanted her to stop him. Lord knew he could use the physical release. But knowing he didn't trust her, would she use sex to try and break through his defenses? Or worse yet, would she feel she owed him something because he'd married her?

Sara tried to think. The kiss had been sudden and unexpected. At the first touch of Jake's lips, her doubts faded…her dreams reawakened. Maybe he could forgive her. Maybe he finally understood why she'd left, why she'd been afraid to stay. She slipped into the world they'd shared once, where kisses and touching could make them one. Jake's lips weren't enough, neither was the sweep of his tongue. She wanted to show him they could recapture the past and forge a future.

She reached for him, her hand finding the taut planes of his back, the richness of the muscles underneath. Running her fingers up and down, she remembered and wanted more.

Abruptly, Jake broke away and growled, "That's enough, Sara."

She didn't understand his terseness any more than she understood why he'd broken away. Trying to rein in her emotions, trying to make sense of the kiss and Jake's reaction, she asked, "What's wrong? We're married Jake. I'd understand if you want—"

"What I want has nothing to do with this. I can't help but wonder if you're willing to use sex to get closer to me, to get what you want."

"And what do I want, Jake?"

"That's what I'm trying to figure out. You got a father for Christopher and security by marrying me. Do you figure your body is a fair trade-off?"

All the breath left Sara's lungs and the room swam. This was more than a lack of trust. Jake's resentment and anger were greater than she ever imagined. "Nothing I tell you will change the way you feel. So you're going to have to figure it out on your own. But maybe you'd better start by deciding if that kiss was a test or a disguise for something else."

She pushed up from the cushion, the strength she'd developed since she'd broken up with Jake taking her up the stairs without a backward glance. She realized now they could never recapture the past. They'd have to start from scratch. The problem was—she wasn't sure how to start at all.

Hearing the key in the lock Wednesday evening, Sara pushed her knitting into the tapestry bag. It had been six days since she'd realized she and Jake had to start from square one. When Jake had gone out of town on business, she'd begun knitting him a sweater for Christmas. It was her way of believing in the future, believing that by the new year she and Jake would have a future. But she'd also made some decisions. The first was—if desire flared between them again, Jake would have to make the first move. She had too much self respect to let something like that happen again.

The second decision of taking a job if it was offered...

Jake came into the living room and plunked his traveling bag by the sofa.

"Did you have a good trip?"

"I'll find out tomorrow after I make some calls." He glanced toward the stairs. "Everything all right here?"

"Just fine. I put Christopher to bed about an hour ago."

His gaze slowly passed from her hair, pinned with a barrette on one side, over her lavender jumpsuit, to the length of her legs. "I'll have to make some time to spend with him tomorrow. I missed him."

So much for easing into the conversation of her getting a job. "I have an appointment tomorrow afternoon, and I've asked Aunt El to look after him. Would you like to keep him yourself?"

"Where are you going?"

"I received a call from a day care center where I had an interview. They want me to come in again."

"I see."

Sara wasn't sure Jake really understood. She'd decided she couldn't center her life around him. She needed to have her own goals. "I might be late. The supervisor said after we talk, she'd like me to stay and see how the facility is run."

Jake shrugged. "Tell Eloise I'll keep Christopher. I'll just make something on the grill for supper."

"You're sure? If you're trying to get something else done, he can be a handful..."

"I'm capable of taking care of my son and making supper. You do it all the time."

Yes, she did. But she'd had three years of practice. She wasn't about to say that and take the lid off Pandora's box again. "Would you like something before you turn in? I made a casserole for supper that I can heat up."

Jake's gaze again passed over her legs and came to rest on her lips. "No. Food doesn't hold any appeal right now." The huskiness in his voice told her that he was thinking about the kisses they'd shared, the desire that hummed between them. But she wouldn't sacrifice her dignity again. She would not be the one to give into desire. Not after what Jake had said.

"Has Christopher had any more bad dreams?" he asked.

"No. But I've been leaving on the hall light." She made herself break eye contact and stand. "I'm glad you're back, Jake. Christopher and I both missed you."

He cocked his head and studied her carefully as if looking for the truth. She didn't want her every word to be suspect. She didn't want to have to watch what she said. So instead of standing there and letting him search, she said, "Good night," and headed for the stairs.

Thursday afternoon, Jake used the pruning sheers on the bushes while he watched Christopher play on the swing. As he clipped the crepe myrtle, he thought about this last trip. Usually, he didn't mind traveling. But this trip, the whole time he'd been away he'd thought about...Christopher—what he was doing, how he was doing it, whether he slept through the night.

"Daddy, look!" The command came from a few feet away.

Jake looked up and felt his heart stop. His son was standing, actually standing, at the top of the sliding board. Jake dropped the shears and his legs ate up the distance in seconds.

Holding Christopher at the waist, he told him, "You don't stand at the top. You could fall. Sit and slide down."

Christopher's brown eyes showed surprise, then defiance. "Don't wanna sit."

"Sit down, Christopher."

"No."

The screen on the porch slammed and Sara came down the steps into the yard. She wore a cornflower blue suit, the same color as her eyes. Her white high heels were simple but showed the curves of her legs to perfection. As she came toward him, Jake took a deep breath.

Seeing his mother, Christopher sat at the top of the

slide looking as angelic as any three-year-old could. Suddenly Jake realized Christopher was testing him, seeing how far he could go. Like any child he was trying to push the boundaries as far as he could.

Sara patted her son's knee. "I have to leave or I'll be late."

"Go ahead," Jake urged, arching a brow at his son. "We're fine."

Doubt flickered in Sara's eyes, but Jake had to give her credit, she didn't voice what she was thinking. She was really trying to let him develop his own relationship with his son. That couldn't be easy for her after having him all to herself.

She gave Christopher a last loving smile and a wave, then walked along the path leading to the front of the house. As the sun shone on her head, red highlights sparkled. With each step, her hips swayed and Jake felt a tightness he recognized all too well. He'd hoped his trip had given him some perspective, but his body didn't know one perspective from the other. He was attracted to Sara and he'd have to live with it.

Christopher slid down the sliding board landing unsteadily on his feet. Running around to the ladder, he climbed to the top again, and promptly stood as if daring Jake to scold him.

So much for perspective.

Four hours later, Jake glanced at his watch then back at the mess in the kitchen. Groceries lay scattered across the counter. Christopher sat on the floor in the midst of strips of unrolled paper towels, plastic containers filled with water from the bathroom sink, and a variety of pots and pans. His son wore one of the lids on his head.

Sara made taking care of their son and the house look easy. It wasn't...unless she knew some secret she hadn't shared. Of course, Jake hadn't let her share much, preferring to learn about his son himself. He'd learned a bookful this afternoon. She was right about Christopher wanting his own way. If Christopher didn't have Jake's full attention, he did everything he could to get it.

The afternoon had been a battle of wills. Jake hadn't been around a lot when Davie was this age. He'd been too busy trying to make detective, trying to make the world a safer place. This afternoon, he'd realized how little he knew about disciplining a child. Davie had been an easy baby, a joyful toddler, an eager first grader. Mary Beth had handled the discipline and when Jake was around, Davie usually cuddled in his dad's lap for a story or simply played within reach.

Christopher was more active, wanting to do or go. He was curious in a way Davie had never been. And when that curiosity was curbed...

Jake recognized his own stubborn streak in his son, but wasn't sure how to deal with it. So he'd done the best he could by warning, cajoling, reasoning. Only Christopher had ignored most of it, doing what he damn well pleased. Finally, Jake had let him, not knowing what else to do, especially after their trip to the grocery store which had been a sheer nightmare.

Jake heard the front door open. He ran his hand through his hair and mentally groaned. Wouldn't Sara get a kick out of this!

He waited for her hoot of laughter or her gasp of surprise. But when she finally appeared in the doorway, she was silent. Christopher ran over to her and hugged her around the knees. His shorts were wet, his hands were sticky, and there was a smudge of chocolate on his forehead from the candy bar he'd picked up at the store and insisted on eating right there.

She crouched down to him, unmindful of his sticky fingers. "Did you have a good afternoon?"

Christopher glanced guiltily at Jake but then bobbed his head.

Sara raised her chin and met Jake's gaze. "Did you have a good afternoon?"

"I don't think 'good' quite characterizes it."

A small smile played on her mouth, and she bit her lower lip.

Jake suspected she was suppressing a grin.

"I'm trying to get supper started," he said gruffly. He didn't like to be laughed at, but he deserved it after this fiasco.

"I'll take Christopher upstairs and help him get cleaned up, then I'll help you with supper."

It seemed like no time at all until Sara and Christopher returned to the kitchen. But instead of adding to the chaos, Christopher helped Sara pick up the pots, pans, and paper towels.

Jake had managed to wipe up most of the water.

When Christopher settled on the living room floor to build with a set of blocks, Jake asked Sara, "How do you do it?"

Turning from the lettuce she'd torn apart for the salad, she asked, "Do what?"

"Watch him and get anything done!"

She didn't laugh as he suspected she might. "It took practice."

He hung a wet towel on the handle of the stove. "I could practice from now until doomsday—"

"Jake, he was testing his boundaries."

"I figured that out. I just didn't know what to do about it." Admitting that was tough for Jake. He was used to knowing what to do, rarely confused about what direction to take.

Sara sliced a carrot into the salad. "I use time-outs with Christopher."

Jake stood beside her, watching her slender fingers. "And they are...?"

"When he does something he's not supposed to do or doesn't listen, he has to sit in a specified chair for three, five, or seven minutes. I set a timer. I should have told you about it, but I thought you'd want to find your own way of dealing with him."

"In other words, you didn't think I'd listen to you."

Sara diplomatically kept silent and sliced a cucumber.

Jake mowed his hand through his hair. "I found out today how different kids are. Because I was a father once, I thought I could do it the same. But each child is as individual as his name."

"Christopher reminds you of Davie." She said it softly, not pressing too hard.

He leaned against the counter. "Yes. But today I really saw them as two different boys. They might look alike, but Christopher is Christopher."

The only sound in the kitchen was Sara slicing the cucumber.

He realized all the things she could say, how she could resent him for not seeing Christopher as unique all along. But she kept silent.

Jake remarked, "He can be a little tornado. I guess you know what works with him."

"Not all the time," she said in a tone that let him know she understood the afternoon he'd experienced.

She was letting him keep his pride, telling him subtly that she didn't have all the answers, either. But where their son was concerned, she knew a hell of a lot more than he did. "Time outs, huh?"

She put down the knife. "Time outs and lots of hugs. You're good with Christopher, Jake."

"Yeah, I guess I'm not too bad. The house was still standing when you got home."

She laughed at his wry humor, and he had to smile back. He also felt compelled to move closer, to breathe in the enticing scent of lingering perfume, to watch her breasts rise and fall with each breath.

Sara saw the frustration leave Jake's face, saw the golden desire flash in his eyes before he moved closer. Her hand, resting on the counter, began to tremble. She and Jake had managed to have a normal conversation. They'd worked together cleaning up and starting supper, as if they shared a common bond, as if they were working side by side like a husband and wife. And he'd realized Christopher was unique in his own right. Maybe now the pain from Davie's death would diminish and he could find joy in this son.

She wanted Jake to kiss her. She wanted it so much she was shaking. But what would Jake's reaction be afterward? The same as the other night?

As his head bent to hers, she knew she couldn't let him kiss her until she found out his motive. Before his lips could touch hers, she whispered, "Is this another test?"

He raised his head and frowned, his voice husky. "I guess I deserved that." Moving away as if her interruption had brought him to his senses, he said, "I'll start the hamburgers on the grill."

Sara wished she hadn't said anything, had let the kiss happen. But she couldn't take that chance, not if she wanted Jake to respect her. She had to start with that.

A few hours later, Sara put Christopher to bed. While Jake read their son a story, she went out on the back porch to enjoy the quiet, to let a bit of peace surround her soul. When she heard Jake's footsteps in the kitchen, she didn't expect him to come out and join her. But tonight instead of heading to his office, he came out onto the porch.

Leaning against the wrought iron railing, he crossed one foot over the other. He looked relaxed, but Sara knew better. Jake never did anything without a reason.

"How did the interview go today?"

The late day warmth still lingered in the air although the temperature had dropped. With Jake standing on the porch with her, the warmth took precedence. "It went very well. I can have the job if I want it when the program director goes on maternity leave in a few months."

"I'd prefer if you don't take the job."

She sighed. "You want me to stay here with Christopher."

"Yes. Is there anything wrong with that?"

"No. But I'd feel better if I'm contributing to our income."

"You don't need to work, Sara. I can support us. It's more important that you raise our son." After a tense silence, he added, "Or do you want a job for other reasons?"

"Like...?"

"Maybe you need to stash some money away in case you want to bail out."

All she could do was reassure him, if he wanted reassurance. These days, she didn't know what he wanted. "I have no intention of bailing out. But maybe you'd like to think I will. Are you hoping I don't stay? Then your responsibility for us would be over. You could say you tried but it just didn't work."

He uncrossed his feet and straightened against the balustrade. "Don't be ridiculous. Now that I know I have a son, my responsibility toward him will never end."

"Yes, you've made that clear. My responsibility for him will never end, either."

"Your responsibilities are different. He needs you with him. And now you can be. You don't have to work."

If she relied on Jake to support them, he'd suspect her motives. But if she took the job, he might resent her even more. "I have to think about it, Jake. I'll let you know what I decide."

"No unilateral decision about Christopher. Wasn't that the deal?"

"And as you told me when you bought the jungle gym, I've listened to you, and now I have to make up my own mind."

Jake pushed away from the railing and was close enough that she could see the tiny scar on his left cheekbone. Instead of angry, his voice was amazingly gentle. "When you make up your mind, try to think about what Christopher needs, not about what's going on between you and me."

She wasn't sure what was going on between her and Jake. But it would be easy to put Christopher first, she'd done that since she found out she was pregnant.

Chapter Five

On Saturday afternoon, Jake's headband caught the sweat as he dribbled the basketball around Nathan, aimed, and shot. The ball danced around the rim, teetered, and fell over the side. Jake swore, grabbed for the ball to rebound, but Nathan was quicker.

He dribbled the ball in front of his opponent. "Playing hard today, aren't you?"

Jake swayed back and forth, ready to guard, ready to jump. "I'm playing like I always play—to win."

Nathan went for the basket, but Jake blocked him, almost knocking them both over as he grabbed for the ball. Nathan stooped with his hands on his thighs and took a deep breath. "Let's say you win and give it a rest."

Jake shook his head. "Uh huh. I need the workout. Getting too old for this?" he needled.

Nathan suddenly stole the ball from his friend and casually dribbled it between his feet. "You played with Oscar, Lorenzo and Joe before I got here."

Jake came around the community center once or twice a week to mingle with the kids, to remind himself how much he had needed a role model at their age. "They're seventeen. No strategy. Now you...I have to use my brain as well as my reflexes when I go against you." Picking up his bottle of water on the sidelines, Jake took a few swallows.

"So, how's the marriage going?"

Jake took another swallow then set the bottle on the ground once more. "Subtle, Bradley. Like an eighteen wheeler. At least with Gillian, she gives me a lead-in before she probes."

Nathan shrugged. "Gillian says you're as tight as a clam on this subject. What gives?"

Jake swiped the ball from Nathan, aimed, and sank it. "Nothing. Sara and I concentrate on Christopher."

Nathan's voice floated over Jake's shoulder. "Twenty-four hours a day? After he's in bed?"

Jake shrugged, as if he hadn't spent more than one hour in his office, so distracted by Sara's presence in the house that he couldn't concentrate. "You know what it takes to be a parent. I'm learning how to handle him." Jake grimaced, remembering Thursday afternoon when he'd lost control of the situation. "And he's learning to handle me."

Nathan grinned. "You mean get away with murder. The girls tried that with Gillian but she was too smart to fall into that trap. We stood together and they realized they couldn't bamboozle either one of us." He paused. "Are you and Sara standing together?"

"We're trying." Jake retrieved the ball and jogged back. He gazed at the building that could use a good sandblasting, the teenagers shooting baskets at the other end of the lot, the few gathered on the asphalt watching the others. "Not many kids here today."

Nathan didn't accept the change of subject. "You can't ignore your marriage."

Jake knew his friend wouldn't give up once he'd started something. "Ignore it? I'm trying to deal with it," Jake shot back. Nathan only pried because he thought he could help, but the prying was irritating nonetheless.

"Have you ever considered how Davie's death affected you?" Nathan asked, his eyes serious.

Silence fell between them. Finally, Jake broke it. "Of course, I have. His death is the reason I quit being a cop, the reason my marriage fell apart!"

"More than that. It made you trust nobody but yourself. It was bad enough being a cop. You had to depend on your gut instinct, your training, your reflexes. But when it came to Davie, even those skills weren't enough."

"So what's your point?"

Nathan shifted on his sneakers, but didn't back down. "You don't give of yourself easily. Your guard is up most of the time."

"I let it down once with Sara," Jake murmured, remembering that one night, when she'd held him, when she'd cried his name in ecstasy...

"Are you giving her a chance now?"

Jake closed his mind to the pictures. "A chance to burn me again? I don't think so. I'm not stupid."

"No, you're not. You're angry. About the way you had to grow up too fast, your mother's death, Davie, your divorce, Sara leaving you at the altar. What's that anger going to get you?"

Jake snapped the ball to his friend and Nathan caught it reflexively. "Protection. Like a bullet proof vest. Don't worry about me, Nathan. I know the score and so does Sara. We're aiming at peaceful coexistence. The fates willing, one day we'll have it." A voice asked, *Peaceful coexistence? Is that why you were ready to kiss her again?*

Jake shut out the voice. The longer he was around Sara, the less she'd affect him.

Nathan dribbled the ball in front of Jake. "Christmas is coming fast."

The comment seemed entirely out of context. "So?" He tensed his arms, ready to move in either direction.

"Maybe it'll bring the peace you want to find. Maybe it will bring even more."

Jake didn't get the chance to mull over Nathan's words. His friend feinted to the left, then the right, and made a basket.

Sunday afternoon, the doorbell rang. Sara stood at the bottom of the stairs and heard the low vibrations of Jake's baritone voice as he put Christopher down for his nap. There was no point interrupting a ritual that was becoming precious to father and son.

Sara went to the door and opened it. A tall man stood there. She'd guess he was in his sixties from the wrinkles on his face and the silver in his dark hair, though his well-kept physique in an oxford shirt and jeans made him look younger.

"Hello there, young lady. You must be the gal who left the message."

"No, I'm—"

He didn't seem to hear her as he smiled sheepishly and kept going, restrained excitement buzzing all around him. "I was out of town on business. Just got back this morning. Sorry to bother you but there was no way I could wait till tomorrow to talk to Jake."

"Why don't you come in, Mr...."

"Just call me Harv." He took Sara's hand and pumped it up and down. "The message said Jake got a lead on Bernadette. I can't believe I'm finally going to set eyes on her after all these years. Just imagine. I don't know if Jake told you, but we were high school sweethearts."

It didn't seem to matter that Sara hadn't left the message for Harv. He probably thought she was Gillian. He was so excited about what Jake had discovered, nothing else seemed to matter.

"We went to school together in Houston. Who would've thought Jake would find her back East."

"You've been looking for a long time?"

"Actually, no. I just got up the gumption a few months ago and didn't know where to start. It was my fault we lost touch. I shipped out with the army. She wrote and I never wrote back. Damn, I was young and stupid and wild. Didn't want to be tied down, I thought."

"Well, Harv, I'm glad you're on your way to finding her."

"I'm unattached now. Been a widower seven years. I just hope she's free, too."

"I hope you find what you're looking for."

"If I find Bernadette, she's all I need."

"I know Jake's good at what he does. If anyone can find her, he can."

"Hello, Harv." Jake had come up behind Sara without her knowing it. "Let's go into my office."

Jake's tone dismissed her. He was going to have to accept the fact she wasn't easily dismissed. "It was good to meet you, Harv. I hope you find Bernadette." She went to the kitchen to start a pot roast for supper.

With the roast in the oven, Sara decided she had enough time to make an apple pie. She'd cut and peeled six cups of apples when Jake appeared in the kitchen doorway. She could tell he was thinking about something, about how to put it to her. He always got that little line on his forehead before he gave her bad news.

Although every nerve in her body was alive and shouting that he was in the same room, she folded the pie shell in quarters and lifted it onto the top of the apples.

"You shouldn't have talked to Harv the way you did."

She left the pie shell lay. "Excuse me?"

Jake kept his distance but jabbed his hands into his pockets. The gesture pulled the already snug jeans even snugger. "Harv is my client."

Trying to ignore the heat creeping up her cheeks, she said, "I know that."

"I give my clients facts. I don't raise their hopes needlessly."

"I don't understand. He said you had a lead. He said you knew Bernadette was back East..."

"Yes, I have a lead. That's all I have. You pumped him up, and now he thinks they're going to be reunited. Even if I do find her, what if she wants no part of him?"

"He was already pumped up when he rang the door-bell. All I did was—"

"Pump him up more. I run my business a certain way, Sara. Stay out of it, okay?"

She glared at him, thoroughly annoyed. "You can poke into my life and tell me not to take a job, but I can't go near your clients? Does that sound reasonable to you?"

Jake stood firm. "Yes. One has to do with our son's welfare, the other one doesn't."

She felt like turning that pie upside down on his stubborn head. "You know, Jake, your rules make sense to you, they don't make sense to me. Maybe you should give me a list, the parts of your life that are safe for me to talk about, the areas I should stay away from."

"Don't be ridiculous."

Slowly and deliberately, she said, "I don't think I'm the one being ridiculous."

Jake took his hands from his pockets. "This is business. I give my clients factual information, and I don't feed their emotions. I find too many dead ends, and I will not give false hope."

"All I did was make conversation!"

His brown eyes were hard. "All you did was interfere. I had to bring Harv back to earth."

She turned back to the pie and opened the folded shell to give her hands something to do. "Fine. I'll stay away from your clients. When the doorbell rings, I won't answer it. Unless, of course, I have your permission. All right, captain?"

"Sara..."

She didn't meet his gaze but crimped the edges of the pie shells, hurt edging out the annoyance she'd first felt.

The phone rang in Jake's office. She felt him hesitate, then move away to answer it. He was effectively trying to keep her pigeonholed, to think of her only in association with their son. There was nothing she could do about that but live with it until Jake decided he wanted her in the rest of his life. She could be waiting a long time.

After reviewing his notes, Jake pushed his chair away from his desk. Harv's former sweetheart didn't drive and apparently didn't work. That made it harder to trace her. He'd found a record of her marriage to a Pennsylvania insurance salesman and the death certificate of that husband. But that's all he'd found. He had a contact on the East Coast checking real estate records. That's all he could do for now.

He heard the buzzer go off on the oven. A few minutes later, Sara went up the stairs, probably to get Christopher up from his nap. Jake sighed. He couldn't take a breath without thinking about her. She was complicating his life, stirring up feelings, let alone hormones he'd thought were inactive, if not dead. They were active all right and very much alive. Confusing as hell. He'd almost kissed her again the other night, and it wouldn't have been any kind of test. Then he remembered what she'd done. He'd remembered that she'd walked out without telling him the truth.

But he still couldn't stay away from her. He definitely couldn't stay away from his son. He shut down the computer and went up to Christopher's bedroom.

Christopher had just awakened. His hair stood up in spikes as he rubbed his eyes. Sara sat on the edge of the bed, picking up books that were scattered at the foot. Before Christopher fell asleep in the afternoons, she let him page through his favorites. Jake marveled at the way she could teach without words, the simple things she did to evoke Christopher's curiosity or instill a good habit. Her son didn't realize it, but Sara was doing everything she could to prepare him to read.

Finally Christopher yawned and scrambled onto his mother's lap. "Where's your smile, Mommy?"

The little boy's question made Jake feel guilty. Sara's nature was bubbly and cheerful. Especially around her son, she smiled a lot and laughed. Right now laughter seemed to be a world away and Jake suspected that had to do with their conversation.

He entered the room and didn't wait for Sara to answer. Conspiratorially, he stooped down to Christopher and whispered in his ear, "I think she left it down in the kitchen next to the pie she took out of the oven. Want me to go get it?"

Christopher nodded solemnly. "Uh huh."

"All right. I'll be right back."

Jake galloped down the steps, went into the kitchen, took a quick glance around and picked up a potholder.

Then he climbed the steps again and went into his son's room, holding the quilted square on his palm in front of Sara. "There it is, Ma'am. Already to put on. It must have fallen off when you opened the oven door." Jake hadn't spouted such silliness in a long time, not since he used to tease and play with Davie. He waited for the familiar stab of pain. It didn't come.

Sara didn't look quite so serious as she played along with his silly scenario and said to Christopher, "Well, look at that smile. I didn't even realize it had fallen off."

When she switched her attention from her son to Jake, he saw the hurt still lingering in her eyes. He never expected his criticism would bother her so much.

Laying the potholder gently on her lap, he said, "Whenever you're ready. I miss your smile, too."

Her gaze questioned him, searching for sincerity. She must have found it because she pretended to lift something from the potholder. She held it to her mouth, smoothing first over her top lip, then the bottom one. Her playful gesture was sensual without her knowing it.

Then she smiled and gave Christopher a hug. "Is that better?"

Her son nodded.

Jake wasn't sure it was better. Her smile packed a wallop, hitting him where he felt it most.

Wednesday evening, when Sara turned the end table light down a notch in Gillian's living room, Christopher didn't stir. Covering him with an afghan from the back of the sofa, she returned to Gillian in her kitchen.

Jake's partner was pouring tea. "It's herbal so it won't keep you up tonight."

Sara sat on a chair and pulled it in to the table. "Thanks for inviting us for supper." Nathan and Jake were attending a budget meeting at the community center. Gillian had invited Sara, Jake and Christopher to dinner. After she'd put Matthew to bed, Christopher conked out on the sofa.

"With the men at the meeting, I figured we'd have some time to talk. If you want to."

Seeing Gillian and Nathan together in their home, watching Jake's relationship with both of them, Sara knew she had nothing to be jealous about. She'd like to have Gillian as a confidante but because of her friendship with Jake that might not be possible.

Sara pulled the cup of tea toward her. "What has Jake told you? About our marriage, I mean."

"That Christopher is his son, that you lied to him and walked out before the wedding. His words, not mine."

Sara picked up the cup, decided the tea was too hot to sip, and put the cup back on the saucer. "I'm surprised you're friendly. You're Jake's friend."

Gillian pulled out a chair and sat across from her. "I'm not making any judgments, Sara. I don't think most people hurt each other intentionally. We all do what we think is best at the time, and we all make mistakes."

"Nathan doesn't think Jake should have married me, does he?"

"Nathan wanted Jake to be sure about what he was doing."

"Jake's always sure about what he does," Sara murmured.

Gillian gave her a wry smile. "You believe that tough guy act?"

Sara sighed. "Sometimes I have no choice. Others..." She thought about that afternoon in her mother's garage when he suggested she keep the vanity, their incendiary kiss, his obvious love for their son. "Jake told me you're psychic. Sometimes I wish I were."

"And sometimes I wish I weren't. At times words and sounds and impressions pop into my head about someone, about something, but I don't know if they're past, present or future. Usually I see a connection to the present."

Sara couldn't keep from asking, "What do you see about me and Jake?"

Gillian took a sip of tea, then put her cup on the saucer. "I don't 'see' anything. I feel a strong connection between the two of you."

"Christopher."

Gillian shook her head. "No. Much more than Christopher."

"I just can't make Jake understand why I didn't tell him..."

"If you love him, eventually he might understand. And if he doesn't, you'll have to make a decision that's right for you and your son."

Sara stiffened in her chair. "That sounds like a prediction."

Gillian shook her head. "Nope. Experience. Nathan

and I had some rough patches, too. I thought he was still in love with his ex-wife."

Relaxing again, realizing Gillian could be a friend, she said, "Tell me about you and Nathan. Seeing you two together gives me hope. You seem so happy."

"We are." Gillian told Sara how she met Nathan, and how they fell in love.

She'd just finished relating how Nathan had proposed when the phone rang. Excusing herself, she went to the living room to answer it. Nathan and Jake returned via the back door as Gillian reentered the kitchen. She looked troubled.

Nathan crossed to her and kissed her on the forehead. "What's wrong?"

"I just received a phone call from a lawyer in Phoenix. When he couldn't reach Jake, he called me. The police department there gave him our numbers. He's looking for the daughter of a client who's seriously ill. He's checked all the databases and keeps hitting roadblocks. So he wants to know if we'll fly down and see if we can help. Before it's too late."

Nathan asked, "Are you taking it?"

Gillian glanced at Jake and he nodded. "Yes."

Jake asked his partner, "When do you want to leave?"

"Nathan, what do you think?"

"I can work at home for a few days and take care of Matthew. If I have to go into the office, I'll call Mrs. Haynes."

"You're sure?"

Nathan put his arm around his wife's shoulders. "I'm sure."

Sara's gaze found Jake's. "We'd better go home so you can pack."

"Is Christopher sleeping?"

"On the sofa."

"I'll get him."

After thanking Gillian for supper, they left. In the car, Jake said, "I don't know when I'll be back."

This was the nature of Jake's work. It gave his schedule flexibility but also immediate demands. "I know. Maybe I'll call Nathan tomorrow and tell him I can keep Matthew if he needs to go to his office."

Jake gave her a quick, sideways glance. "Mrs. Haynes is like a grandmother to Matthew. He's used to her. But Nathan might be glad to have a back-up." After a pause, Jake said, "I don't like leaving you alone again so soon after the last time."

"It's all right. I understand."

Jake hesitated a moment. "You can reach me on my cell anytime. If there are any problems here that I can't fix long distance, don't hesitate to call Nathan."

"And I have Eloise. Don't worry about us, Jake. Christopher and I are used to being on our own."

"You aren't on your own any more." Jake's voice was husky.

His concern felt so good. It warmed her, made her heart feel lighter. Maybe time would lead to forgiveness and togetherness.

While Sara put Christopher to bed, Jake packed. She remembered clothes he might need that she'd stacked in the laundry room. After she kissed her sleeping son goodnight, she went to get them.

She pushed open the door to Jake's bedroom. The high, king-sized four poster bed was the main focus of the room, though the armoire and nightstands were pieces of quality, too. A cedar chest sat at the foot of the bed across from the fireplace and easy chair.

Jake tossed a few pairs of socks into the travel bag. "I've written down the number of the hotel, too."

Sara laid two knit shirts on the bed, remembering one cherished night, remembering the love they'd shared. Jake looked up, saw her expression and his jaw tightened. His gaze passed over his clothes, the bed, Sara. The atmosphere between them hummed with all the tension that had surrounded them since she'd returned. She didn't know what to do or what to say.

Jake broke eye contact and resumed packing.

Sara took a few deep breaths. "I won't go Christmas shopping for Christopher until you get back."

He gave her the hint of a smile.

She stared at his large hands rearranging clothes, pushing over a shirt to fit in the shaving cream. His hands were so gentle, so caressing, so wonderfully tactile. Even just his fingertip on her cheek could create excitement. Before she changed her mind, she said, "I'll miss you."

His smile faded. He threw the top of the bag over the bottom and zipped it. "Don't forget to put the security system on when you're out and at night."

"I won't."

"If you forget the code..."

They'd covered all this the first time he'd gone out of town. "I won't forget it, Jake. I gave the combination to Eloise."

She'd obviously made a mistake telling him she'd miss him. Nothing she said brought them closer together. Time. She just had to wait. "I'll make breakfast before you leave tomorrow. Then Christopher can say good-bye."

Jake nodded.

Sara went to her room, closed the door, and sat at the vanity Jake had encouraged her to keep. He did care. She just didn't know how much.

I'll miss you.

Sara's gentle voice echoed in Jake's head, and his body tightened. Each day became more of a battle, a battle against his emotions, a battle against his desire for her.

Staring out the window into the blue of the sky and the white of the clouds, he didn't think he'd ever felt more weary in his life. Sara seemed to be softness and goodness, but he'd thought that once before and he'd gotten torn apart. Keeping his focus on Christopher was the only way to maneuver through this marriage...the only way.

He glanced over at Gillian who had closed her eyes and was napping. How long had it been since he had a good night's sleep? No wonder he was so tired.

Jake closed his eyes, but didn't feel the calmness and peace of slumber. He saw Sara's face.

Sara's knitting needles worked in and out, in and out, as she tried to make progress on Jake's Christmas present. The sweater had become a symbol of the love she felt for him. The shade of hunter green would look wonderful with his black hair and deep brown eyes. She'd found a shirt the perfect color to blend with it.

When the phone rang, Sara reached for it eagerly.

"Sara, it's Jake."

He'd been gone two days and she'd done a lot of thinking. "Hi. How's it going?"

"I called to give you another number. We're staying in Grand Rapids now. Gillian has a sense the woman we're looking for is about an hour and a half from there near a lake."

"So you don't have any idea when you'll be home?"

"I'm hoping in a couple of days. But I can't say for sure."

She wanted to tell him she missed him but he always seemed to back away when she said she cared about him. Yet there was a quality in Jake's voice she didn't recognize, that urged her to ask, "Are you all right?"

"Fine. The mattress at the last hotel was as hard as concrete."

She smiled at his description. "Did you sleep at all?"

"Enough. How's Christopher?"

"Growing. I took him to the pediatrician Gillian recommended. He's grown an inch and weighs three pounds more than he did before we left Wasco."

"Everything's all right, though? I mean, you just took him for a check-up."

"Everything's fine. I, uh, wanted to tell you I've come to a decision about the day care job."

"Oh?" He sounded wary.

"I think you're right. It would be good for me to be home with Christopher. But, Jake, I would like to finish up my degree in early education so I can eventually teach. I could go part time."

Jake was silent for a few moments. "You don't have much to finish up."

"No. Eloise said she'd keep Christopher while I'm at class."

"And you want to start course work in January?"

"I'd like to."

There was a long pause. "We can discuss it more when I get home. I have to go now, Sara. We're making an early start tomorrow."

Something urged her to say, "Take care of yourself."

"You, too."

Jake's good-bye was husky, and Sara wondered if he didn't miss her just a little.

The key missed the lock and Jake tried it again. This time it slipped in and the lock turned. As soon as he closed the door, he was aware of Sara's presence. Her blue gaze met his and she smiled, a smile that made his head throb along with other parts of his body.

Sara rose from the sofa. She wore a rose caftan that molded to her body as she moved toward him. Geez! Just what he needed right now. He hadn't been able to get her out of his head the whole time he'd been gone. Even when he'd tried to come up with a Christmas list for Christopher.

"Welcome home."

He dropped his suitcase by the stairs. "I guess Christopher's in bed."

Her smiled flagged slightly. "About an hour ago. If I'd known you were coming home, I would have kept him up. Was your trip successful?"

He hadn't called because they'd barely had time to catch the flight out tonight instead of waiting until morning. He'd felt this drawing back to L.A., to Christopher and Sara that he'd never felt before. "Thanks to Gillian, it was. She's incredible. The woman we found flew back to Phoenix to see her father, and we flew home."

Sara stepped closer to him, and he could smell the bubble bath she used. The scent often lingered in her bathroom after she'd gone to bed. Once in a while when he passed it to gaze at his sleeping son, he'd stop and take in the flowery smell. It was stupid, really. Thank goodness he had his own bathroom off of his bedroom. That's all he'd need—finding Sara naked some morning...or night...or anytime in between.

"Jake?"

Her soft voice sounded far away. But she was very close...too close. He needed some air. "I've been cooped up in planes and hotel rooms too long. I'm going out for a run."

"Now?"

"Yes, now. You don't have to wait up." He lifted his suitcase again and took it up to his room.

Sara didn't know what she expected this time with Jake's homecoming, but she'd hoped for more than she'd gotten. On top of Jake's remoteness, she sensed some-thing was different...even wrong. A huskiness in his voice, a fatigue in his tone and demeanor she'd never heard or seen before. What he needed was a good meal and a massage to loosen the knots from traveling. Ooh, would she like to give him a massage!

Sara Donovan, behave yourself.

She sighed. Unfortunately, she would. She had no choice.

She'd put the finishing touches on a tray of cheese and crackers when she heard Jake return. She hurried to the living room before he could go upstairs. What she saw made her run to him. "Jake, what's wrong?"

Chapter Six

Bent over, with his hands on his knees, Jake's face was flushed, his breathing ragged. When Sara took hold of his shoulder, it burned her hand. Had he gotten overheated while running?

She slipped her arm around his waist. "Let me help you."

He started for the sofa. "I don't need help." He'd almost made it there when he stumbled.

Ignoring his protest, she curled her arm around his waist. "You're scaring me, Jake. Let me help you."

His gaze burned into her, but he nodded. "All right."

At the sofa, he sank down and laid his head against the back. She sat next to him and felt his forehead. He was sweated but there was a burning heat underneath that hadn't developed from his run. Taking his wrist between her fingers, she took his pulse.

"What are you doing?"

"I've had emergency training. Just keep quiet for a minute." His pulse was strong but much too fast. "What's going on, Jake?"

He shook his head, then looked as if he regretted the motion. "I've felt so damn tired the last few days."

"Has your throat been scratchy?"

He glanced at her sideways. "How'd you know?"

"The tone of your voice has been different. Don't move," she commanded. "I'm going to get the thermometer."

He straightened then held his head. "I don't need—"

"I'm trying to find out what you need. I need to find out exactly what condition you're in. Now stay put or I won't pick you up when you fall on the floor." Her threat was empty, and they both knew it. But Jake didn't argue. It was probably the picture of him falling on the floor that kept him still. He hated to appear weak in front of anyone.

She raced upstairs and found the thermometer she kept in her bureau drawer. She had a sixth sense where Christopher was concerned. She could tell how high his fever was just by touching him. With Jake... She suspected it was higher than even he imagined. It had to be to put him in this condition.

Downstairs, she slipped the thermometer into his mouth. Her fingers touched his lips and the heat in his gaze came from more than the fever. Shaken, but knowing she'd have to get past this strain between them to care for him, she said, "I'm going to boil water for tea and get you a glass of orange juice. If that fever is as high as I think it is, you need to get liquids into you."

"I hate tea."

"Coffee's out because of the caffeine. The tea is herbal. It will help settle your stomach."

"How do you know my stomach needs settling?" He'd taken the thermometer out of his mouth to ask.

"You're looking at the cheese and crackers as if they're going to hop up and bite you. The man I know can eat anytime, anyplace, anywhere." She took the thermometer from him and stuck it back in his mouth. "Don't talk till I come back."

He gave her a defiant glare.

Rolling her eyes, she went to the kitchen, suspecting he was going to be one recalcitrant patient, worse than her son when he was sick. Unfortunately, she couldn't give Jake a coloring book and crayons to entertain himself. He'd always been a man on the move, but he was probably going to feel worse before he felt better.

When she returned to the living room, his eyes were glassy. The thermometer apparently had beeped and e held it loosely in his hand. Slipping the thermometer from his fingers, she read it—103 degrees.

He took it from her and blinked so he could focus. "That can't be right."

She laid it on the coffee table. "You're sick, Jake. You probably have a virus that has to run its course. But if we don't get this fever down by tomorrow evening, we should call the doctor."

"I don't need a doctor," he growled.

"Then cooperate with me."

"And what's that supposed to mean?"

She stood and planted her hands on her hips. "Don't fight with me and do what I tell you."

He gave her a disgruntled grimace. "All I need is a good night's sleep." Edging to the rim of the couch, he tried to stand and slumped back down.

"You need a good night's sleep, but you need fluids

and aspirin and maybe a sponge bath, too."

That suggestion brought his eyes to hers. "Forget it."

"At least let me help you get upstairs."

After a silence, he said with resignation, "All right. The room spins every time I move."

Progress. Maybe.

Jake pushed up, levering himself on the arm of the sofa. Sara's arm circled his waist, and she took his weight. He was hot, and damp, and so extremely male. She loved being this close to him. She loved helping him. He hated it.

"Are you ready?" she asked gently. She felt his nod and they moved toward the stairs.

Jake was a tall man, lean, but pure muscle. In the upstairs hall, she stopped and propped against the wall with him for a moment.

"Are you okay?" he murmured.

Catching her breath, she said, "I'm fine. Just a little farther."

When Jake collapsed on his bed, Sara breathed a sigh of relief...until she realized he was shivering. "Do you have a pair of pajamas?"

He dropped his head into his hands. "Never wear them."

Searching in his dresser drawer, she found a pair of flannel jogging shorts and a T-shirt.

"Sara, I'm fine."

"You can't crawl into bed in clothes that are sweated from running. Do you want to get better or catch pneumonia?"

"You're worse than a nurse," he grumbled as he tugged his shirt over his head. "Throw me the clothes."

"I'll go get the tea and orange juice." She laid the clothes beside him on the bed.

A short time later, the glassware on the tray jiggled as Sara carried it into Jake's room. He was lying in bed, the covers pulled over him, his eyes closed. She knew he needed to rest, but he needed to get the aspirin and fluids down first. She placed the tray on the nightstand and sat down on the bed next to him.

Opening his eyes, he saw her and the tray. "Sara..."

"If you don't listen, you'll be setting a bad example for Christopher."

"That's blackmail."

"That's the truth."

"He's not even awake."

"If you'd expend less energy arguing with me and more doing what you're told, you'd be sleeping by now."

"I never realized how stubborn you can be," he muttered.

She raised her brows. "Which do you want first? Juice, water, or tea?"

When he reached for the glass of water, his hand shook.

She handed it to him with the aspirin. "Are you cold?"

He nodded. "Even the covers aren't helping."

"Will you let me sponge you down?"

"No way, lady," he snapped as he gulped down the aspirin and grimaced.

"Does that hurt your throat?"

"I'll survive."

"Life is about more than surviving, Jake. Work on that cup of tea. I'll be right back."

"Stubborn and bossy, too," he mumbled but did as he was told.

She'd always loved the idea of a fireplace in the bedroom. Tonight, a fire would help break Jake's fever. She'd spotted kindling and logs in the shed outside. Loading the carrier she found by the fireplace downstairs, she wondered just how bossy and stubborn Jake would let her be. She'd rather crawl in beside him and warm him with her body, but if he wouldn't agree to a sponge bath, she doubted he'd agree to that.

He was huddled under the covers again when she brought the wood into his bedroom. His eyes were closed. She'd laid the fire and touched it with a match when he opened them.

"This should help you get warm. If it doesn't, I'll get you another blanket."

"Sara, you don't have to do this."

Standing at the foot of the bed, she rested her hand on one of the posts. "We're married, Jake. Caring for each other is part of that, at least for me. That's one of my rules to go with all the others you made up." She nodded toward the tea. "Try to get the rest of that down."

As she got ready for bed, she stayed dressed in her caftan, but added socks. It seemed wise. After picking up a novel she'd started one night when she couldn't get to sleep, she checked on Christopher, then returned to Jake. His room had warmed up and she didn't expect she'd need a cover. He looked as if he'd fallen asleep.

The arm chair in the sitting area of the room was heavy, but she managed to nudge it with her knee away from the fireplace and closer to the bed. Then she turned off the lights and settled in it, ready to keep her vigil. She dozed, waking when she heard Jake tossing and turning. Hurrying to his side, she felt his forehead. It still burned her hand. Stoking the fire, she resettled in her chair.

A few hours had passed when she awakened again. In the shadows, she sat beside Jake and felt his forehead. Beads of perspiration told her the high fever had broken. Crossing to the dresser, she took out another T-shirt and pair of shorts, then went to the kitchen and poured apple juice. It wouldn't burn like the orange juice when it went down his throat.

Beside Jake once again, she held the glass out to him with two more aspirin.

He didn't argue and managed to drink half the glass. That was a good sign. But they had another hurdle to cross.

"You can't sleep in those clothes. You'll get more chilled."

Even in the dark with only the embers of the fire casting shadows around the room, she could feel Jake's gaze on her. He tried to sit up straighter, but dropped his head back on the pillow. "Forget it."

"C'mon. I'll help you."

He tried to sit up again. Sara was quick and tugged his shirt up his arms and over his head. Her fingers grazed his ribs. With him bare chested, she wished she could lay her cheek against his chest rather than hand him his shirt. Unfolding the shirt to make it easier for him to put on, she gave it to him. Their hands touched and she saw him wince. "I know, you're skin hurts when you have this kind of fever."

He let the comment stand. "I can take care of my shorts."

She let him try, but his strength seemed to give out when he'd pushed them to his knees. He swore.

"Jake, it's dark. I'm certainly not going to see anything if that's what you're worried about."

"I'm not worried about anything. Go ahead. Drag them off." She tried to slip the shorts off without flipping back the sheet. That wasn't too hard. But she couldn't help him put the fresh ones on that way. Ignoring his grunt of disapproval, she turned back the sheet and started his shorts up his legs, pretending not to look at anything else. Pretending, because she knew what Jake looked like. His long legs, powerful thighs, and...

She took a deep breath.

He sat up, and his hands closed over hers. She went still, her gaze finding his face in the dimmest of light. "This is too dangerous," he said, his voice husky. "Go back to your room."

Dangerous for him, or dangerous for her?

He went on in a raspy voice, "Every time you breathe I can see that damn drape outline your breast. No wonder I'm sweating. Go back to your room, Sara. We'll both sleep better."

Had he been watching her when she thought he was sleeping? She ignored his warning. "Move over to the other side of the bed where the sheets are dry. The next time you wake up, I want to take your temperature. If it's down, I'll go back to my room. For now, I'm staying."

She tilted her head. "Unless you want to throw me out." They both knew he was in no shape to do that.

"You're going to get a stiff neck in that chair."

"It's really not bad."

"Sara..."

"Right now, Jake, I'm a lot stronger than you are."

"You want to test it?" he growled.

Her heart raced. Even in the condition he was in, if she challenged him, she had no doubt he'd meet it. "No." Handing him the glass of water, she ordered, "Drink."

He took the glass and managed to get most of it down. Then he moved over the other side of the bed and laid back on the pillow. Finally his eyes closed. Sara breathed a sigh of relief and went downstairs to refill the water glass.

As she stepped back into the room, Jake was muttering in his sleep. The fire had almost burnt out. After she added kindling, she stoked it back to life and added a log. Jake's muttering became louder, more intelligible.

"No, no, not Davie. Oh my God, nooo..." He tossed first to the left, then to the right.

Sara hurried to him. He'd turned his face away from her. She didn't want to wake him, and not knowing what else to do, she gently rubbed the middle of his back. He stopped moving restlessly, and his muscles seemed to relax. She kept rubbing. She didn't know how long she soothed, how long she rubbed his spine, the broad span between his shoulders. After he'd been quiet for some time, she stopped.

His hair curled around his ear and lay at the nape of his neck. She couldn't help wanting to touch it. Brushing it away from his ear, she put a tender kiss on his cheek. Then she went back to her chair to keep the vigil.

The sun was creeping over the window ledge when she awoke again. She stretched and yawned, then sat up and looked over at Jake. To her surprise, he was sitting on the edge of the bed. "Going somewhere?"

"Yes. To the bathroom. The fever must be down because the room's standing still."

She approached him and touched her hand to his forehead. "Not quite as bad. But I want to take your temperature anyway to make sure."

He pushed himself off the bed and took hold of the nightstand.

"Jake..."

"I'm fine," he muttered as he used the wall to make his way to the bathroom. She held her breath until he reemerged still on his feet. But barely. When he got to the bed, he stretched out, his breathing labored.

"Was it really worth the effort to do that by yourself?"

He closed his eyes. "Yes."

She sighed and reached for the thermometer. When she touched it to his lips, he opened his eyes. They bored into her, and she wondered what he was thinking.

His temperature was down to 101. She handed him aspirin and the glass of water. After he drank it, he said, "Go to your room and get some sleep."

"Only if you promise to call if you need me."

"I'll call."

He wouldn't, but she realized that at this point her presence could keep him from resting. With nurselike precision, she straightened his covers. "You try to sleep, too."

He nodded.

She left his door open, hoping she'd hear him if he got out of bed. When she crawled into hers, she wondered if he'd resent her for the care she'd given him, for seeing him weaker than he wanted to be. It didn't matter if he did because she'd do it all again. She loved him.

Jake's head throbbed when he woke up, but not nearly as badly as it had the night before. He'd seen the worry in Sara's eyes. He'd been worried himself. He never got sick!

Suddenly, he remembered the nightmare. An old one. More than the nightmare, he remembered Sara's hand on his back. He'd almost shrugged her away but it had felt so good...calming. He'd almost stopped breathing when she'd brushed the hair from his neck, when she'd kissed him. Had that been a dream? His overactive libido working even in his sleep? He'd watched her resting in that chair and as bad as he'd felt become aroused by it.

She'd fought to take care of him last night. Why? Did he dare believe she really cared? That she hadn't come back into his life for convenience or to make her life easier? Why hadn't she fought like that four years ago? Why hadn't she stood her ground and told him she was pregnant? If she'd loved him, she would have. If she'd loved him...

Damn! He was getting sucked in all over again because of a little kindness. He'd better get his guard back up and fast. He hated feeling weak. He hated feeling defenseless. Must be the flu.

The door to his room opened and Sara came in carrying a tray. Christopher was right behind her but waited at the threshold. She smiled at Jake. "He wanted to make sure for himself that you're all right."

Jake mustered up the best smile he could. "I'm getting better. But you'd better stay clear until I can come downstairs. I don't want you getting sick."

His son's brown eyes got wider. "Mom says Thanksgivin's soon. You gonna be okay then?"

Thanksgiving was only ten days away. "I'm sure I'll be fine until then."

Sara said, "Play in your room for a few minutes till I take your dad's temperature."

"Okay." Christopher scampered off.

"He's a good kid."

"And a better patient than you are." She held out the thermometer to him. "Here. You can have breakfast after you take it."

This time he didn't argue with her. The scrambled eggs looked light enough to float down his throat and his stomach rumbled.

She laughed. "Good. You have an appetite."

He had an appetite for more than her food.

Jake checked the thermometer before he gave it to her. "It's only 99. I'm better already. Good thing, too. I have calls to make, paperwork to go through..."

"Jake Donovan, don't you even think about stepping out of this room, let alone bringing work up here. If you don't behave today, I'll call Nathan."

Jake couldn't suppress his smile. "And just what do you think Nathan's going to do?"

"Sit on you if he has to. There's no reason you can't stay in bed and relax today. I called Gillian and she said she'll be in, and she'll handle any emergencies that come up."

"You had no right to—"

"Tell her her partner was a little under the weather? I don't need rights to do that. A secretary would have done the same thing."

Sara was right. He didn't know why he was being so argumentative. Maybe because she was invading every area of his life, and he felt crowded. After a lengthy pause, he asked, "Truce?"

She smiled. "Does that mean I don't have to call Nathan?"

"It means I appreciate everything you did for me last night."

Today, Sara wore jeans and a T-shirt that were every bit as appealing as the caftan that had swirled around her last night. Her smile slipping away, she came closer. "You had a nightmare last night. Do you remember it?"

Jake blanked out the pictures that were ready to flood his head. "Yes. It's the same one I always have. The car in flames, Mary Beth screaming..."

"It might help if you talked about it."

Jake hadn't talked about it to anyone, except when he'd told Sara about it, then Nathan and Gillian. "There isn't anything to talk about. Davie died and it was my fault."

"Jake, you can't still believe that."

"The bomb was in my car, meant for me. It was my fault. If that had been Christopher, you'd blame me, too."

She sat on the bed next to him and covered his hand with hers. "Are you so sure of that? Your loss was as great as your wife's. I can see how much you love Christopher. I can imagine how much you loved Davie. Some thug killed your son. You have to forgive yourself for being a cop then, or you'll never have any peace."

The pain in Jake's chest became so great, his throat tightened painfully. Sara's hand on his was like a lifeline, a way out of the pain. He studied their hands. She couldn't be his lifeline. He couldn't need her that much. If he did, and she left, too...

Sara looked at him with such compassion, he wanted to pull her down beside him on the bed, kiss her rosy lips, stroke her soft skin, breathe in every part of her. His pulse thudded and so did his head, bringing him back to reality with a jolt.

He reached for the tray she'd set at the foot of the bed. "I'd better get started on the eggs. If you have things to do downstairs, don't worry about me. I'll remember to take more aspirin in a few hours." Knowing he sounded gruff, he settled the tray on his lap.

Sara stood. "I'll check in a little while if you need anything. But I won't bother you if you're resting."

When she left his room, he wanted to call her back. But he didn't know what he'd say if he did. So he kept silent.

The following evening, Sara reached for Christopher's block at the same time as Jake. Their fingers brushed and the heat between them had nothing to do with the blaze in the living room fireplace. Jake's gaze had been on her all evening, as if he was trying to figure something out. They both chose a different block to add to their son's architectural masterpiece that was about ready to topple over. When Jake had awakened this morning, his fever had disappeared. He'd worked with Gillian in their office most of the day. By supper, he'd looked tired but his complexion now had the ruddy color of renewed health.

Suddenly, Christopher's building collapsed on the coffee table. The three-year-old just giggled. "Do it again."

Sara glanced at her watch. "Nope. It's time for bed."

Glancing first at Jake and then at his mother, he accepted her verdict. "Can Daddy read two stories tonight?"

Christopher had missed Jake while he was gone and the two days he'd been sick. Sara waited for Jake to answer.

"Help me gather up the blocks, then we'll pick out two books."

A smile lit Sara's heart. Jake was getting good at handling Christopher.

She enjoyed the ritual of putting their son to bed. It was a time when she felt closest to Jake. But tonight, even while he was reading with Christopher nestled in his lap, she felt his gaze on her now and then in the same searching way.

After they'd tucked in their son and Sara preceded Jake down the stairs, she wondered what was coming. Sitting on the sofa, she waited.

Jake crossed to the fireplace and stared into the leaping fire. When he finally turned and looked at her, she felt she could go up in flames as easily as the extra kindling laying on the hearth. "I've been thinking about what you said, about going back to school. If that's what you want to do, it's all right with me. Do you want me to pay for it, or will you use the proceeds from the land in Arizona?"

His question took her aback. "I'd like to save that money for Christopher's education."

"From what you've said, it'll probably be a drop in the bucket. Besides, he won't need it. I'll be paying for his education."

"Both of us have the responsibility for his education. Both of us should be working together for all of our needs."

"Because California's a community property state?" His brown eyes were unreadable.

"I don't understand what you mean."

"What's mine is yours and what's yours is mine?"

She hadn't really thought about all that. "Yes, I guess. Though the land in Arizona might not sell for a while...if ever."

"It could be a very long while," Jake agreed, still giving nothing away.

"I don't know what you're getting at, Jake. It's a little late for a prenuptial agreement. I'm surprised you didn't have someone draw one up before the wedding." She couldn't keep the hurt from her voice. Standing so she'd feel as if she were on more equal footing, she tried to keep her voice calm. "I have a job at the day care center if I want it, but you don't want me to work while Christopher's at home. I'd like to go back to school, yet you're going to resent paying for it. Do I have that right?"

Jake mowed his hand through his hair, a sure sign of frustration. "No, I won't resent paying for it, not if we're working toward the same goal of building a life together."

What in heavens name did he think she was trying to do if not build a life with him? The suspicion he'd voiced before hit her with renewed force. "Do you still think I married you for security?"

He came closer, almost within touching distance. She could smell the trace of aftershave he'd used that morning, could see the shadow line of his beard, could feel the tension in his body as all that was past, present and maybe future vibrated between them.

His eyes darkened as he said, "I think you were tired of trying to make ends meet, tired of working and trying to give Christopher attention at the same time, tired of not capturing your dream. Marrying me solved all your problems."

The spark of anger inside her flared. She was tired of his suspicions, tired of feeling as if she was guilty of some terrible wrong. "Solved them? Let me tell you, Jake Donovan, my 'problems' as you put them seemed a cinch compared to living with your distrust. Maybe this Christmas you should ask for a heart to replace that block of stone in your chest." As soon as she said it, she knew she'd gone too far.

Jake reached for her and crushed her against him. "Stone? You think any part of me is made of stone? Let's see what you think after this."

His mouth covered hers as his arms tightened her against him. The hardness she felt was hot and pulsing with life. Not stone...but male and heat and desire. His embrace and his kiss demanded she respond. Should she meet his demand or would she regret it if she did?

Chapter Seven

Jake's lips opened on hers, his tongue broke the seam of her lips and thrust inside. The strength of his passion melted doubts, the fervor of his desire engulfed her. She'd waited so long for him to hold her in his arms. Reveling in being where she most wanted to be, she curved her arms around his neck and laced her fingers in his hair. It was longer than she'd ever seen it. She loved its vitality, its thickness, the slide of it through her fingers.

His tongue stroked hers, dashed against the roof of her mouth as if he couldn't taste her fast enough. Angling his head, his hands passed up and down her back. She wanted him as much as he wanted her. The fullness in his jeans tempted her, urging her to become bolder. While she stroked his jaw with one hand, she rubbed her breasts against his chest. His groan vibrated through her.

He broke their kiss, and she protested. But he'd only stopped to edge his fingers under her sweater and yank it over her head. His gaze went directly to her breasts.

Their rosy peaks showed through the lace cups. Quicker than she could blink, he unhooked her bra and held one rough palm to each breast. She loved the feel of his calluses on her skin. On the sensitive skin of her breasts, the stimulation was almost more than she could stand. She closed her eyes to absorb the wonder of his touch. Suddenly, she felt the wet, rough texture of his tongue sliding against her nipple, and she moaned. When he did it again, her knees buckled. He held her as they slid down to the floor.

Palming her breasts, he kissed her hard, again and again and again. Sara couldn't keep her world right side up. But she was aroused enough to know she wanted his skin against hers, his body filling hers. She reached for the buttons on his shirt, trying to concentrate on slipping one after the other out of their holes. After she managed the last button, she slid her hand across his chest.

Jake laid her on the floor and unsnapped her jeans. She reached for his. "I want you, Jake. It's been so long..."

Her voice penetrated the haze. For the first time since he'd kissed her, he stilled and gazed into her eyes. She saw anguish there and didn't know why. "What's wrong?"

He swore viciously and looked away. "This is wrong."

"We're married, Jake."

His voice was gravelly. "Sara, the way things are between us...what happens if we have sex and regret it?"

She sat up, conscious of her nudity, but more concerned with what Jake was thinking. "You seem sure that would happen."

He stared into her eyes. "When I make love with you, Sara, I don't want to have doubts. I don't want to wonder if you told me about our son so I could take care of you both. I don't want to wonder if you're pretending something you don't feel."

He was as vulnerable as she was, maybe more so because he was so good at hiding it. "And what about you, Jake? How am I supposed to know what you feel if you don't tell me?"

"I'm telling you now."

"What do you feel?"

For a moment, she thought he wouldn't respond, that he'd button his shirt and walk away. Instead he ran his hand across his forehead, then answered her. "I want you, Sara. Plain and simple. My body and my mind remember what we shared. But I won't be that blind again. I need to be sure we're going to make it before I give you more than my body."

"I can't separate my mind from my body," she said softly. "I loved you then and I love you now."

Anger creased his brow and vibrated in his words. "If you'd loved me, you wouldn't have left. My father left. In her way, my mother left. That's not love. Maybe you'd better decide what love means to you. Because to me it means sticking together no matter what."

"I promised I'd stay when I married you."

He shook his head. "Promises can be broken. That old adage is true that actions speak louder than words. We haven't been together long enough for me to trust in your promises this time."

Her eyes filled with tears, but she also felt a glimmer

of hope. He'd been honest with her. He'd unlocked his feelings and let her see his vulnerability. Because of that, she believed they could have a good marriage. She'd prove to him he could trust her or she'd die trying.

Avoiding his gaze, she reached for her bra. Jake turned away and snapped his jeans. The awkwardness between them couldn't get any worse. She slipped her sweater on and ran her fingers through her hair. Sensing Jake had closed himself off again and further discussion about their marriage wouldn't solve anything, she searched for something tangible to talk to him about, to keep the connection between them.

"Thanksgiving is coming up soon. What would you like to do?"

Slowly, he buttoned his shirt. "Did you have something in mind?"

"I'd like to ask Aunt El, of course. Do you think Nathan and Gillian would like to join us?"

"Nathan is flying Gillian's mother in for the holidays."

"They could all come here," she suggested.

Jake studied her, as if she were a puzzle he couldn't quite put together. "You sure you want to take on a dinner that size?"

"Thanksgiving is about family and extended families. I think we'd all enjoy it."

"Do you want me to ask Nathan and Gillian?"

"No, I'll do it. And maybe next week we could go Christmas shopping for Christopher?"

"We did say we'd do that."

He wasn't pushing her away, even after sharing what

he had. That gave her so much hope her heart almost flipped over in her chest. "I'm going to prove to you that you can trust me, Jake. I'm going to prove I love you."

He met her eyes and cocked his head.

She felt more naked than she had a few minutes ago when her clothes had lain in disarray on the floor.

His voice was gentle as he said, "We'll have a large Thanksgiving dinner if that's what you want, and we'll go Christmas shopping together. But you and I both know things won't change overnight."

She wasn't that naive. But she was filled with more hope than even she thought was possible. Christmas was a time for wishes to come true, and she'd always believed in Christmas magic. Maybe she could show Jake it was time for him to believe, too.

As Jake walked by shelves of toys the day after Thanksgiving, he actually felt happy. He'd hardly remembered the feeling of lightness, the wonder of laughter, the simple joy of smiling often. Sara had made Thanksgiving Day a holiday to remember. He was grateful to her for that and a lot more—giving him a chance to get to know his son, championing their relationship...taking care of him when he was sick. It had been a long time since anyone had taken care of him. He'd hated the feeling of powerlessness at the time, but...

In his mind's eye, he could see her sitting in the light of the fire by his bed. He needed a way to thank her, and he might have found it. Yesterday Eloise had reminded him about Sara's birthday on December nineteenth. He and her aunt in a quiet moment had discussed how difficult the holidays would be for Sara this year without her mother. That's when the idea had hit. A surprise party for Sara. Christopher would love it, too, though Jake knew better than to tell him about it before the day of the party.

Sara walked down the aisle of the toy store beside Jake. Remote control cars lined these particular shelves. Jake picked up the demonstrator model and set it on the floor. He pushed a button and it ran over Sara's toe.

He grinned. "Sorry."

Sara teased, "Do you want that for Christopher or yourself?"

He looked as sheepish as a five-year-old. "Maybe we should get two. Then we could race them."

His crooked smile melted her. They were almost through the toy store and their cart was stocked full of books, games, a stuffed panda bear, a backhoe practically as big as Christopher, an electronic device that could help a child learn to read, a baseball mitt, and a variety of stocking stuffers.

"Maybe you should ask Santa for one."

Jake's gaze was hot on hers. "I've got a few things on my list that are a cut above remote-control cars."

"A Ferrari?" she managed.

"How about an old fashioned Christmas with all the trimmings?"

"That would be my wish, too," she said softly.

The heat between them sizzled as Jake came toward her. He stopped directly in front of her. If he leaned forward, their bodies would touch. "You made yesterday special. I wanted to thank you."

Her light jacket seemed heavier, the temperature in the store higher. "No thanks are necessary."

"You did most of the work. Gillian's mother couldn't stop raving about your pumpkin pies."

"She was being polite."

"Yeah, so were me and Nathan when we almost ate a whole one ourselves."

Heat crawled up her cheeks. Thanksgiving Day had gone well. There had been laughter and hugs and wishes on the wishbone. "I'm glad you enjoyed it. Gillian's mom and Aunt El got along great. They're going to have lunch together next week. Did you notice how good Christopher was with Matthew?"

Jake's eyes narrowed and he leaned away.

"I just mean I think he misses being with other children. I'd like to look around for a preschool a few hours a week if you don't mind."

Jake picked up the car at her feet and returned it to the display. "In Wasco, I guess you put him in the same day care center where you worked."

"It was an ideal situation. I could be around him and work at the same time."

His brows hiked up. "Ideal?"

"You know what I mean, Jake. At least when I went to work, I didn't have to leave him with a stranger. I took him with me, and I knew the women who were taking care of him."

"And you think he misses being with other kids?" In a lower voice, almost to himself, he added, "Sometimes kids aren't good for each other."

She knew he was thinking of the gangs of kids who

got into trouble. "Christopher is three. He needs other children to learn how to share, to learn how to make friends, to learn how to win and lose at games."

Jake's stance became more relaxed. "You do always think about what's best for him, don't you?"

"I hope so."

Jake added one of the remote control cars to the basket. "All right. Tell me the truth. Did I go overboard here?"

Sara put her finger thoughtfully to her chin and carefully sorted through the merchandise in their cart. "I think you've made good choices. If we can get out of the store without adding anything else, you did just fine." The golden lights in Jake's eyes warmed Sara and encouraged her. Thanksgiving and tonight had brought them closer together.

As Jake pushed the cart into the aisle, he said, "I forgot to tell you. I found Harv's high school sweetheart."

"You did? Where?"

"The real estate records led us to her. She'd bought a cottage at Nags Head after her husband died. No landline. She has one of those untraceable buy-as-you-go phones. Not much contact with anyone. But Harv flew out before Thanksgiving. He called this morning to tell me he was bringing her back with him."

"What do you think will happen?"

"That's anybody's guess. They both might have changed a lot in all these years."

"Or maybe not so much."

Jake's sideways glance told her he was thinking about the two of them, not Harv and his sweetheart. She and

Jake hadn't changed, not in the ways that mattered. Now all she had to do was convince him.

Sunday morning after breakfast, Sara carefully lifted an ornament from the carton and examined it. The tiny wooden rocking horse barely covered her palm.

Jake turned from the tree where he'd attached strings of lights. "That should do it."

"Can we put stuff on?" Christopher asked.

"Sure can." Jake peeked over Sara's shoulder. "That looks like an old one."

Jake's aftershave teased her, his long, tall body in back of her sent awareness of him through every fiber of her being.

"Most of them are. Christopher and I had started our own collection, but these are Mom's." She handed the rocking horse to her son. "Hang it wherever you'd like."

"Whatever you're baking smells good," Jake commented, his breath fanning her ear.

"Cranberry bread," she managed.

He reached around her and took an ornament from the box. When he hung it on the tree, she watched the play of muscles under his T-shirt. Trying to concentrate on decorating for Christmas rather than Jake's attributes, she reached for the felt-wrapped item. "Look what I found, Christopher." She unfolded the green fabric. "It's our Christmas angel."

"Lemme see."

Sara held up the gold metallic angel with the slim chimes dangling from her gown.

"Where are we gonna put her?"

"I think the back porch might be best."

"So she can see Santa coming," Christopher added.

"Santa?" Jake asked with a grin.

"Uh-huh. We hang her outside and whenever Santa is in the area, she chimes."

Jake's grin broadened. "I see. I'll find a hammer and nail and we'll see if we can find the right spot."

Sara and Christopher waited for Jake on the back porch while he found what he needed in the shed.

On the porch, he tapped a nail into the edge of the eave and held out his hand for the angel. Sara gave her to him, and Jake slipped the ring onto the nail.

"All set. Just waiting for some Christmas magic." He leaned close to Sara and whispered in her ear. "Or the wind."

She swatted his shoulder playfully.

Jake tweaked the tip of her nose. "You let me know when you hear Santa. I'd like to get a glimpse of him."

"Me, too," Christopher agreed.

Sara planted her hands on her hips. "You don't have to see him to know he's around. When you hear the Christmas angel, you only have to believe."

The timer went off in the kitchen. "Now that's a sound I do believe in," Jake remarked. "Something good is coming out of the oven. C'mon, sport. Let's get back to decorating that tree while your mom gets the bread."

Jake took his son's hand and led him inside.

Sara wanted Jake to believe in the Christmas angel because everyone deserved a touch of magic in his life—especially Jake. She remembered the smile on his face as

he tweaked her nose. They were growing closer. Someday soon he'd trust her again and then their marriage
could really begin.

On the nineteenth of December, the trays of sandwich
delicacies, cheeses, and vegetables filled the bottom
shelves of Jake's refrigerator. He put two liters of soda on
the top shelf. He and Christopher had just made a trip
to the grocery store to pick up everything.

"Balloons now?"

Once Jake had told his son they were going to deco-
rate with balloons for his mom's birthday, Christopher
had thought of nothing else. "Okay, buddy. I'll blow
them up. You can help put them where they look good."

The doorbell rang. Jake frowned. He'd cancelled his
appointments for the afternoon. Fortunately, Gillian had
convinced Sara to go shopping. Eloise wasn't due with
the cake until five.

Pushing the pack of balloons in front of his son, Jake
said, "Pick out the colors you like and we'll start with them."

Christopher grinned and reached for a red one.

As Jake walked through the living room, the scent of
pine, the nativity set on the corner table, the pillar candles,
boughs and shiny balls on the mantel, made him smile. Sara
sure had a knack for decorating. She had a knack for a lot of
things—making his house feel like a home among them.

When Jake opened the door, a delivery boy stood
there with a floral arrangement. "Delivery, sir, for Sara
Donovan."

A card stood on a holder higher than the flowers. Jake gave the boy a tip and took the arrangement. He didn't hesitate to look at the card.

"Happy birthday, kiddo. Enjoy. Love, Mark."

Mark. The friend from Wasco. The friend Sara had dated. Why the hell had he signed the card "Love?"

Close friends do that, the logical voice in Jake's mind told him.

The not-so-logical voice worried, *How close?*

Maybe the guy still carried a torch. He obviously remembered details of her life like her birthday.

Sara hadn't mentioned her birthday. Not once. Well, if Eloise hadn't reminded Jake, these flowers sure would have, and he'd have felt like a fool. Even now... He read the card again and looked at the arrangement.

Carnations and evergreens. How ordinary. Sara deserved roses and gardenias and orchids and... Jake set the flowers in his office and called, "Christopher. Come here. We have to go out again."

The little boy came running. "Why?"

Jake stooped down and smiled at his son. "Because we're going to find your mom a whole bunch of flowers. And balloons that fly. What do you think?"

Christopher grinned and took Jake's hand. "Now."

"Yes, now. We might have to go to more than one flower shop." He scooped his son up in his arms. "We're going to give your mom a birthday she won't forget."

Sara stood on the porch with Gillian before she opened the door. "I really enjoyed this. I haven't been shopping with a friend for a long time." She lifted the large shopping bag filled with packages. "I'm just afraid I splurged."

"You bought a dress for Christmas that Jake's bound to like and a few accessories. That is not splurging. Besides, that white dress was designed with you in mind. Your coloring is perfect for white. I'd fade in with the dress."

The white silk with the delicate gold braid around the collar and cuffs was special. Other than her wedding dress, it was the prettiest garment she'd ever purchased. Maybe she'd given in to the impulse because today was her birthday and only her Aunt El knew about it. She hadn't told Jake because she didn't want him to feel obligated to buy a gift.

"Would you like to have supper with us? Or is Nathan expecting you?"

"Nathan's always expecting me." Gillian's eyes twinkled. "But I'll see him soon enough. Come on. You can model the dress for Jake."

"Oh, no. I think I'd rather surprise him on Christmas." Sara opened the door and stepped inside.

Several voices called, "Surprise!"

Christopher came running to her. "Su-pise, Mommy. Happy Birfday!"

Sara dropped her bag and hugged her son. The scent of flowers was strong in the living room. As she looked around at Nathan, Aunt El, and Gillian's Mom, she realized every available surface held a bouquet or basket of flowers. When she saw the vase of yellow roses, tears welled up in her eyes. Besides the roses there were day lilies, poinsettias, mums, even some exotic-looking flowers she'd never seen. Helium balloons flew in bunches toward the ceiling in the corners of the room. She stooped over to hug Christopher again and tried to compose herself.

Feeling a hand on her shoulder, she straightened. Jake's brown gaze held hers. "Happy Birthday, Sara."

The tears rolled down her cheeks and she couldn't manage a word.

Gently, Jake brushed the tears away from her cheeks. "C'mon now. You've got to say something or Christopher will think we didn't do a good enough job."

"Did you do this?"

"I had some help. Wait until you see the cake Eloise baked."

"The flowers are lovely, especially the yellow roses."

He took her hand. "I'm glad you like them."

Sara gazed down at their entwined fingers and loved the feeling of her hand in his. He tugged. "You have presents to open. Come see what everyone has brought you."

Sara had dreaded today. Without her mother, she would have skipped another birthday. Then Gillian had asked her to go shopping. Now this... The tears resurfaced.

Jake lowered himself beside her on the sofa as everyone found a seat, commenting on Sara's surprise. The couch was plenty long, but his hip lodged next to hers, his jeans brushed the fabric of her slacks. Her breaths came faster as Jake picked up a package from the coffee table and laid it on her lap. "This is from Christopher."

Sara removed the blue, stick-on bow from the shoe-box. Jake had probably found the box for Christopher and from the way the bow was positioned, her son had attached it. She lifted the lid.

One of her son's prize stones sat in one corner. It was shiny and black, about as large as a golf ball. Taking it out of the box, she set it in her palm. "Thank you, honey. I'll put it on Nana's vanity so I can look at it often."

Christopher pointed to the folded piece of paper in the bottom of the box. "Open that."

Sara lifted the paper and opened it. The picture was a finger painting, mostly blue and green with a blob of yellow. "How pretty!"

Christopher explained, "It's the sky, an' grass, an' the sun."

Sara gave her son a huge hug. "I like it very much. We can hang it on the refrigerator."

As Gillian took Matthew from Nathan, she said, "Open the pink one next."

Sara tore the paper from the large gift box. Inside, she found a tooled leather pocketbook. "Oh, my, Gillian. It's beautiful!"

"Actually, I narrowed the choice down to two, and Nathan made the final decision."

Sara turned toward Jake's friend. "You have excellent taste."

He grinned and his cheeks flushed. "Gillian taught me everything I know. At least about shopping," he added with a wink for his wife.

Gillian's mom handed Sara a basket filled with different types of teas. "Gillian told me you enjoy unusual flavors."

Sara was touched by the woman's thoughtfulness. "I'll try one at breakfast. Thank you."

Next, Sara unwrapped a box from her aunt. It was a powder blue jogging suit, the type of outfit she liked to wear to lounge in for the evening. Sara went to her aunt, hugged her and kissed her. "You're so good to me," she murmured.

Eloise whispered in her ear, "I promised your mom I'd watch over you. You're the daughter I never had."

Settled once again on the sofa, Sara brushed the wetness from her cheek.

Jake leaned forward and carefully lifted a large, flat box, placing it on Sara's lap. "This is from me."

As she pulled the bow from the box, her fingers trembled. Jake helped her push the paper from the box. Lifting the lid, she stared at ten different poses of Christopher in various shapes and sizes. It was a montage of their son swinging in the back yard, getting a drink from a water fountain, running in a nearby park, licking an ice cream cone. One picture after another of a happy little boy.

Sara could only think of one thing to show her appreciation. She threw her arms around Jake's neck and gave him a sweetly tender kiss. She didn't expect his arms to go around her, but they did. She didn't expect his hold to tighten, but it did. She didn't expect his lips to part, or the depth of the kiss, or the heat curling in her womb as he kissed her long and hard in front of the guests gathered to celebrate her birthday. When he finally broke away, he looked a little dazed himself.

She suddenly felt awkward with everyone looking on, smiling broadly. "Thank you," she murmured. "I love it."

"Daddy took lots of pictures," Christopher supplied.

Jake cleared his throat. "I have files of shots I didn't use in the frame. I can make put them on CD's."

With her heart still thudding in her ears, she wasn't sure what to say or do next.

Eloise stepped into the silence. "Time to eat. Everything is ready in the kitchen. And don't be shy. Jake bought enough for three birthday parties."

Nathan stood first. "I'll try to make a dent."

The others laughed and followed him to the kitchen, Christopher holding little Matthew's hand and guiding him in the right direction.

Jake stood and offered Sara his hand. She took it and smiled. Jake smiled back. Her heart took an excited leap and she felt truly happy.

Two hours later, Nathan and his family left. Eloise cleared one of the trays, packing leftovers into a plastic container. Sara snitched a pickle from one of the trays. "Jake thought of everything, didn't he?" she asked her aunt, still amazed he'd gone to so much trouble.

"I offered to help him plan, but once I reminded him of your birthday, all he wanted me to do was bake the cake."

He hadn't remembered on his own. That wasn't so surprising. Yet once her aunt had reminded him, had he felt obligated to throw her a party? Jake took his obligations seriously.

Christopher ran into the kitchen and stopped at the table, chocolate cake crumbs decorating his upper lip. Jake came in after him. "I told Christopher he could have one more pretzel, then it's time for bed."

Jake's gaze found Sara's. He crooked his finger at her and his expression was serious. "I want to show you something."

Sara followed him to his office where he switched on the light and motioned to the flower arrangement on the desk."

"Jake, you already bought me a roomful of flowers."

"These aren't from me."

His deep voice sent shivers down her spine. She flipped open the card and read it. Jake was watching her closely.

"Does he buy you flowers often?"

There was no point evading Jake. She had nothing to hide. "Usually on my birthday. Sometimes on Valentine's Day."

"You're married now."

"I know. Mark knows. I emailed him, telling him about our marriage, thanking him for sending the boxes I couldn't fit into the car. Jake, I told you before that Mark and I are friends. Just as you and Gillian are friends." She laid the card on the desk.

His smile was wry. "Somehow, it doesn't seem the same." Stepping closer to her, he asked, "Will you email him again?"

Her pulse raced, the room got hot, and every nerve in her body came alive with Jake so close. "That would be the polite thing to do." Trying for a light tone, she teased, "I could email you, too."

He tipped up her chin. "I'd rather have the kind of thank you you gave me after you opened your presents."

The pad of his thumb traced her upper lip so gently, so sensuously, she trembled. He murmured, "Happy Birthday, Sara," a moment before his lips sought hers.

It was a possession, a branding, a desire to change this marriage of convenience into something more. She surrendered to the possession, gave to it, encouraging it, encouraging Jake to take more, want more, trust more. She responded to each stroke of his tongue, as her body melted into his.

"Sara, do you want me to freeze some of the cake? I can...Oh. Sorry."

Jake broke away, and Sara opened her eyes in time to see her aunt scurrying out of the room. But this time, when she gazed into Jake's eyes, he didn't move away. In fact, his hand still rested on the small of her back.

"We have to put Christopher to bed." His voice was husky with the desire they'd shared.

"Jake, thank you for the flowers, the present, the party."

"You're welcome."

The gentle touch of his hand on her back, the golden lights in his eyes, the small smile on his lips told her more than words that he hadn't planned her birthday out of obligation. He cared. And maybe soon that caring would become love.

Chapter Eight

"Fifteen. Sixteen. Seventeen." Sara counted slowly, giving Christopher time to find what he considered a good hiding place. He loved to play hide and seek, especially upstairs where he could slide under a bed or behind a drape.

Drapes and a bed brought Jake's room to mind. Maybe soon she'd be sharing it with him, maybe soon they'd truly be husband and wife. Her birthday party last night had been proof that he cared—and maybe more than cared.

No longer hearing Christopher shuffling into a place to hide, she finished her counting. "Eighteen, nineteen, twenty. Here I come, ready or not."

Sara peeked outside the bathroom where she'd waited. She suspected Christopher might be in his favorite hiding place, but in the name of the game she looked carefully around his room. "No Christopher," she said in a loud voice. Stopping at the door to her bedroom, she called, "Christopher, where are you?" and heard a giggle.

Her guess was correct. Going to the walk-in closet, she opened the door. Slowly, she separated clothes on the rod to peer behind them. "Christopher's not here, either. Maybe he's in his dad's room."

She heard the giggle again.

One side of the closet held blouses, skirts and sweaters. Underneath them stood a round wicker clothes hamper. Her son had wedged himself behind it, but his feet protruded.

"Why, I think I see a sneaker that doesn't belong in here." She wiggled his foot, and he giggled again. "I think I see a stocking, and a leg, and..." She pushed the hamper out of the way. "There's Christopher!"

When she tickled his tummy, he laughed and said, "You found me, Mommy."

She lifted him out of the corner. "You bet I did. I'll always find you. And just in time, too. Teddy told me he's ready for his nap."

"He did not."

She tickled Christopher again and set him outside the closet. "Did, too. Go to the bathroom, then I'll read you a story."

Sara was aware that her son was growing out of nap times. Sometimes, she'd peek in and find him paging through a stack of books. Others, he'd be running his cars over his pillow or talking to Teddy. Many days she found him fast asleep.

She'd read him a story, kissed him, and partially closed his door when the doorbell rang. When Jake answered it, she heard voices, both male and female. Gillian had left for the day. Maybe she'd forgotten something.

Suddenly, Jake's voice came up the stairs. "Sara. Can you come down for a few minutes?"

When she descended the steps, Jake, Harv, and a pretty woman who looked to be about Harv's age were standing in the living room. Harv was grinning from ear to ear. "I wanted you to join us because I want to ask you and Jake a favor."

Sara crossed to Jake and stood beside him.

"But, first, I want to introduce you to Bernadette."

Sara extended her hand. "It's nice to meet you."

Bernadette, a tall redhead with beautiful green eyes, gently gripped Sara's hand. "Harv told me how you assured him Jake would find me and how your words kept him going." She gave Harv a loving smile.

Sara glanced at Jake. He frowned and she realized they both remembered how he'd scolded her the last time Harv was here. "Harv thought I was Jake's partner that day."

"I'm sorry I mistook you for Jake's partner. I've never met her. But it's much nicer that you're Jake's wife. It'll make my idea more attractive, I hope."

Jake motioned to the sofa and they all sat. "What idea is that?"

"Bernie and I are getting married. We've wasted enough time. We want to do it as soon as possible and in style. How would you two like to fly to Las Vegas with us tomorrow? I know it's short notice, and Christmas is less than a week away, but it would only be overnight. You can be our witnesses at the ceremony. We'll have a nice dinner and stay overnight and fly back the next morning. What do you say?"

Sara thought Jake would turn down Harv's offer right away, but instead he seemed to be thinking about it. He turned to Sara. "You're finished shopping and baking, right?"

"I have some wrapping left. That's about it. Why? Do you want to go?"

"You didn't get a honeymoon."

Her mind went into overdrive. "You mean...?"

"I mean, it would be nice to get away overnight and relax before the holidays. If you think Christopher won't mind staying with Eloise."

"Oh, I don't think he'll mind. Not just one night. We can ask him when he gets up."

"Harv, we're honored you asked us. Can I call you in a couple of hours and give you our answer?"

"Well, sure. That'll be fine."

After Jake and Sara saw Harv and Bernadette to the door, Jake closed it and turned toward her. "Would you like to go? Harv kind of put us both on the spot."

"It would be nice to spend some time alone with you—without Christopher, I mean. We could concentrate on us."

Jake took her hand, held it in his palm, and smoothed his fingers over the top. "I'd like to concentrate on us."

Her heart soared. This was the moment she'd been waiting for—Jake willing to believe in her again...in them. *Las Vegas, here we come.*

The bellboy smiled when he looked at the tip Jake handed him. "Thank you, sir. Anything else you need..."

"We're fine. Thank you." He closed the door on the young man.

Sara picked up her garment bag to hang it in the closet. Jake took it from her. "I'll do that."

His leg brushed hers, khaki slacks against her tunic top and leggings. They'd been touching more lately, not jumping apart, letting the sensations linger—at home, in Harv's private plane, as they checked into the hotel. It was tantalizing and frustrating at the same time.

Jake crossed to the closet and hung up the garment bag. "We have two hours before the ceremony. What would you like to do?"

Sara's gaze met his across the two double beds.

His brown eyes sparked with gold, and she knew they were both thinking the same thing. But the first move had to be his. She wouldn't ask him to make love to her. She wouldn't beg for his trust.

"We could look around," she suggested. "Take a walk. I've never been to Las Vegas."

"At night, it's lit up like a Christmas tree. All year round. But we can walk around now if you'd like."

Sara took in everything—the desert, the marquises, the people on the street. She smiled at passersby, and they smiled back. Jake guided her past resorts, restaurants, and wedding chapels. When they returned to the room, Sara sank down on the bed. "Whew! This is some place, isn't it?"

He smiled. "Nice place to visit but you wouldn't want to live here?"

She smiled back. "Something like that." She paused, and chose her words carefully. "I'd like to get a shower. Uh..."

"You go ahead. I'll get one when you're finished." He picked up the ice bucket on the dresser. "I'll go get some ice. Would you like anything to drink?"

"Juice of some kind if they have it."

He nodded and went out the door.

She let out a pent-up breath. They were being so careful with each other. Like they were on their first date. Maybe they were.

Sara had packed light—the Christmas dress for the ceremony and dinner, jeans and a blouse for their return trip, and...a satin nightgown and robe. Wishful thinking perhaps, but just in case...

Taking shampoo, brush and comb from the pocket of the garment bag, she took the robe from its hanger and went into the bathroom. In the shower, she let the hot water beat on the back of her neck. She hadn't realized how much tension she was holding there. When she finished showering, she used the hair dryer on the wall to dry her hair.

She opened the door and stepped into the bedroom.

Jake was sitting in the chair by the window, rifling through a newspaper, sipping at a cola. His terry robe lay on one bed. "I got you orange juice. They..."

Gazing at her above the newspaper, his eyes became dark and dangerous.

She cleared her throat. "I...uh...can put on my make-up at the vanity out here if you want to shower."

He folded the newspaper in half and laid it on the

table. When he stood, she backed up. But it didn't matter because he picked up his robe and came toward her anyway. Stopping in front of her, his gaze started at her feet and slowly moved up her body until it lingered on her lips, finally her eyes.

"If I kiss you now, we'll never make it to Harv and Bernie's wedding."

Her hands trembled and her knees wobbled. "They'd be disappointed."

"Unfortunately, that's true." He slipped by her, but stopped at the threshold of the bathroom. "It would be a good idea if you're dressed when I come out."

Sara sank down on one of the beds. She had the feeling this was going to be an evening she'd never forget.

She'd applied make-up, dressed, and was clipping a gold barrette in her hair when the bathroom door opened. Making herself stay facing forward, she took a peek at Jake in the mirror. His hair was still damp, brushed to one side, tendrils dangling on the nape of his neck. The V of the robe's lapels displayed a matt of black chest hair. The hem of the garment stopped at his thighs, powerful thighs that even in shorts didn't look as sexy as they did below the robe.

When he crossed to the closet, she slipped into the bathroom again and closed the door. There, she waited until he had time to dress. She felt foolish, but also awkward, hopeful, and excited, too. Finally, she opened the door.

Jake was tying his tie when she crossed to the dresser.

She opened her purse and dropped her lipstick inside. Suddenly she felt Jake close, his hand on her shoulder.

He gently turned her toward him. "You look beautiful." He traced the gold braiding on her collar. "Like a Christmas angel."

"And you look very handsome in your suit. It reminds me of *our* wedding day." Still a bit damp, Jake's hair tumbled over his forehead. Sara couldn't keep herself from touching him, from pushing it over his brow.

He took her hand and brought it to his lips. They were warm and sensual on her palm. "We have a wedding to attend." His murmur was a husky reminder that they were in Las Vegas for a reason. They'd have to deal with their feelings and desires later.

Sara marveled at the circus atmosphere in Las Vegas. Weddings were a breed unto themselves—from the drive-up window where couples exchanged vows in their car to the chapels where Elvis impersonators performed solos. A limousine had met them at the airport when they arrived. Jake had told her on the plane that it was Harv's usual mode of transportation when traveling.

Sitting beside his fiancée, Harv pointed to the bottle of champagne chilling in its magnum. "We'll break that open after the ceremony." He took his fiancée's hand and put it on his knee. "It was only a month or so ago these folks got hitched. Got any advice, Jake?"

Jake shook his head. "I'm no expert."

Bernie addressed Sara. "I guess what I'm worried about most is both of us being so set in our ways, we'll drive each other crazy."

"As long as you love each other, you can get past that. You can compromise," Sara answered, believing it.

Harv squeezed Bernie's hand. "Havin' doubts, darlin'?"

Her eyes found his. "Not about loving you."

His expression got serious. "Then I agree with Sara. The rest will settle itself. We've waited too long not to be together now."

As usual, Sara couldn't tell anything from Jake's expression, if he was thinking about the last four years or the next four.

The chapel they entered was less gaudy than a few she and Jake had seen that afternoon. It was no bigger than Jake's living room. The inside was painted white. White doves and silver bells hung from the ceiling. Five wooden benches flanked the left and the right. An aisle with a red runner divided the room and led to the dais where a podium stood.

The minister met them at the door. Harv shook his hand and introduced him to his bride-to-be and their witnesses. The limousine driver presented Bernie with a bouquet of daisies and orchids. With her cream taffeta, street-length dress, her upswept red hair, and her sparkling green eyes, she was a stunning bride.

The driver handed Sara a smaller bouquet of daisies and roses. Her hand trembled as she took it. In a way, she felt as if she were getting married all over again.

Sara stood beside Bernie while Jake took his place beside Harv. The minister's words as well as the vows Bernie and Harv exchanged were similar to those in Sara and Jake's ceremony. As the couple put rings on each other's fingers, Jake's gaze met Sara's. She thought she saw sadness in the depths of his brown eyes, but she wasn't sure. She wanted to see joy and hope and the love she felt for him. But he was still guarding himself.

When Harv and Bernie gazed into each other's eyes and kissed, the love and passion between them was obvious. It was a few moments until they broke away from each other, smiling sheepishly. After Harv thanked the minister, he gathered his new bride close to his side, grinned, and said, "Let's celebrate! Wait until you see the dinner I've set up."

Back at the hotel, the maitre d' showed them to a table far enough from the band to be private, but close enough to enjoy the music. Harv pulled out a chair for Bernie while Jake did the same for Sara. Another bottle of champagne sat beside Harv's chair.

"I hope you like lobster tail and filet mignon. Cherries jubilee for dessert, so save some room."

Harv flew his plane all over the United States in conjunction with his consulting business in setting up computer networks. His stories about clients and the glitches he ran into often kept conversation flowing during dinner. Except...

As Sara dipped chunks of lobster into butter and transferred the fork to her mouth, she'd catch Jake watching her...intently. He spent more time on his steak than the lobster, and Sara couldn't keep her eyes from his strong hands and agile fingers as he used the steak knife and brought the meat to his lips. She felt so close to him, yet so far away. It was a strange sensation.

As he put down his fork and pushed his plate away, his knee brushed hers under the table. Sara didn't move.

His gaze collided with hers, and she held her breath. The intensity there practically stopped her heart. He pushed his chair back and stood.

"Harv, if you and Bernie would excuse us, I'd like to dance with my wife."

Harv chuckled. "I understand. You'll know when dessert's arrived by the flames over here. But if you're too engrossed in what you're doing, we'll understand."

Jake extended his hand to Sara. She took it. He kept his palm on the small of her back as he guided her to the dance floor. Only a few couples were dancing to the slow mood music. Sara had never danced with Jake before. They'd always spent their time talking or hiking in the canyons. Dressing up and going out hadn't been important to either of them.

But tonight, dancing seemed to be the perfect thing to do.

Jake took Sara's right hand as he slipped his arm around her waist and drew her toward him. He held her close. Very close.

"What flames are Harv talking about?"

"You've never eaten cherries jubilee?"

She shook her head and her chin brushed his lapel.

"Basically the cherries are cooked with brandy then lit until the flames dissolve. That gets rid of the alcohol and leaves the flavor. Then the cherries are served over vanilla ice cream. A simple dessert with a fancy name and a fancy way of making it. They light the cherries right at the table. It's some show."

She laughed. "I guess we will know when they serve dessert."

Sara moved in a small box, her steps following Jake's as if they'd danced together often. His breath whispered against her brow as he said, "You were distracting me at dinner."

"I was?"

"Um hmm." Leaning back, he didn't loosen his hold. "The way you eat lobster is sinful."

She felt a blush crawl up her neck. "I like lobster."

"I could tell. You ate it slowly, savoring each morsel. And when the butter coated your lower lip..." He brought their bodies into even closer contact. "I could only think about kissing you. Letting you enjoy me like you were enjoying that lobster."

She went hot, then cold, then hot again. His words were exciting her, making her want him even more than she already did. She had the feeling he knew it. "I watched you cutting your steak."

"And?"

"And I remembered how capable your hands are, how gentle, how...arousing."

"Why, Sara Donovan, I think you're trying to turn me on."

"And what are you trying to do?"

He made a slow circle on the small of her back, pressed his thighs against hers, and teasingly caught her ear lobe with his lips. If he hadn't been holding her, her legs would have buckled.

After suckling her ear lobe, he placed a gentle kiss on her neck. "I guess I'm trying to tell you I don't want us to sleep in separate beds tonight. How do you feel about it?"

Feel? She felt as if she were suspended somewhere between heaven and the sublime. He wanted her. He wanted her in his bed and in his life. "I'd like to share your bed with you, and anything else you want to share."

She felt him stiffen. "Sara, just because we sleep together doesn't mean all our problems are solved."

"What are our problems, Jake?"

He trailed his finger down her cheek. "Damned if I know right now. All I can think about is undressing you, kissing you, touching you. How fast do you think we can eat dessert?"

His chagrin and frustration made her smile. "I'm pretty good at downing ice cream. Three minutes tops."

"If you eat ice cream too fast, it can give you a headache."

"Then I'll be sure and take at least five minutes. Because, Jake, I'm not going to have a headache tonight."

The flare of desire in his eyes was more potent than any flames on a dessert. He kissed her with a slow lingering tenderness, creating an ache inside her that could only be satisfied one way, soon, in Jake's bed.

When he lifted his head, fire leapt between them. Sara knew she was going to get burned, but she didn't care because she'd decided to give anything to Jake that he wanted. In giving, she would find his love.

He glanced over her head. "The waiter is standing at the table. We'd better go back."

Sara didn't remember much about dessert. The ice cream was cold on her tongue, the cherries warm and sweet, but not as sweet as Jake's kiss. He kept watching her, her lips particularly as she spooned in the dessert. She tried to keep her mind on the conversation, but the best she could do was add a short comment here or there.

Finally they were finished. Harv set a time for them to meet the next morning, and then she and Jake were riding up to their room in the elevator. He was standing a few inches away from her. She wanted to touch him, to feel the heat, to make sure it was still there, but she didn't feel that freedom with him yet. Maybe after tonight...

Jake slid the card into the lock, opened the door, and turned on the light. Sara didn't know what to do next. Jake had made himself clear when they were dancing, but now...

He slipped off his suit jacket and tossed it over the chair. Then he opened the top button of his shirt and tugged down his tie. It hung loose around his neck. He mowed his hand through his hair and then looked at her. That look. She saw the desire, but something was missing, something they'd lost.

He crossed to her and stood before her, the nerve in his jaw working, his cologne wrapping around her, the swell of tension between them rising to a screaming pitch against the background of silence. "I want you, Sara. I want you so badly I couldn't touch you in the elevator because I knew we wouldn't have made it back to the room. I don't want to scare you. I don't want your needs to get trampled because—"

Jake had been a patient, gentle lover...the first time. She laid her finger over his lips. "I'm not afraid of you, Jake."

He sucked in a breath and crushed her to him. His lips were anything but patient. His tongue speared into her mouth taking her breath away. While he kissed her, his hands found the zipper at the back of her neck. It scraped down the track. There was a harshness about the quickness of it. But there was nothing harsh in Jake's kiss, just unleashed passion that he'd denied for too long. She reached for the buttons of his shirt, as eager to touch him as he was to touch her.

With a groan, he pulled away. She let her dress fall from her shoulders to the carpet. The expression on his face was pained. She'd worn nothing but her bra and lacy panties under the lined dress.

He stared at her, his cheeks flushed by the heat bursting between them. "I remember everything about you. I remember..." He passed his hand over the slight roundness of her belly, the swell of her hips. "Having Christopher has made you more beautiful."

His fingertips so light on her skin sent thrills through her. She reached for his belt buckle, but he stilled her hands by covering them with one of his. "You really haven't been with anyone else?"

His question hurt her because he was still doubting whether or not she'd told him the truth. All she could do was reassure him again. "You were the first, Jake, and the only one."

Closing his eyes, he brought her hands to his lips and kissed her fingertips. Then he wrapped her arms around his waist, kissed her again, hard, with a possessive intensity that was raw need. She passed her hands up and down his back, appreciating the strength, loving the feel of him. She felt a shudder rip through him. Apparently her touch was as potent as his.

Unhooking her bra, he backed her up toward the bed. Then he swept her into his arms and laid her down. She watched him swiftly undo his belt buckle and drop his pants. With a shrug his shirt landed on the floor. When he skimmed off his briefs, she just stared. Jake was powerful and male and looking at her as if he wanted to devour her. She held out her arms to him.

He came to her and skimmed her panties down her legs. When he brought his mouth to her breasts, she cried out in pleasure. His hands teased and taunted, increasing the ache inside her until loving Jake became foremost in her mind. He tested her for her readiness with his fingers. And then...

His heat was gone, so were his lips, his hands. "Jake?"

She heard the nightstand drawer open.

He ripped open the foil packet and prepared himself.

"Jake, I'm on the pill. As soon as we decided to get married, I—"

"Better safe than sorry." His voice was husky with need but clear in his message. Christopher would be their only child. He hadn't changed his mind about bringing children into the world. She had expected that, that's why she'd gone on the pill. But it was the rest of the message that stabbed her heart. He still didn't trust her.

Before she had time to think about it, before she could feel the full extent of the pain, he rose above her and kissed her again. This was the man she loved, the man she wanted to love for the rest of their lives. She opened her arms and her heart to him. When he surged into her, the pleasure was so intense, she gripped his buttocks to urge him deeper. He thrust and thrust again until she cried out, flying over the edge of desire into joy yet anguish too—because Jake was still protecting himself from loving her.

As soon as he heard her cry, Jake let himself go. But even then, as he found completion, they weren't complete. They were still two separate people, lovers now, but not fully loving. How could she prove to Jake he could trust her? How could she earn his love?

Chapter Nine

Jake sorted through the mail, giving the business letters to Gillian. "Here's something for Sara. I'll be right back."

He went to the kitchen and sniffed appreciatively. Chocolate chip cookies. She was baking them so Christopher could leave a few for Santa Claus—she was trying to make Christmas Eve a special night.

Sara transferred cookies from the racks on the table to a can. Coming up behind her, Jake breathed in the scent of her shampoo mixed with a more womanly scent that turned him on instantly. It didn't take much these days. With Sara, it never had. Three nights ago in Las Vegas, they'd come together in passion. He'd felt changed in some way ever since.

Brushing her hair behind her ear, he dropped a string of kisses along her collarbone. "Hey, pretty lady. I hope you're going to leave one out for my snack."

He felt her tremble as he pressed against her. She was so responsive to him. Sleeping with her, reaching for her in the middle of the night, had become a habit in a few short days.

Sara turned in his arms. "If I give you one, you'll want six. I know you and chocolate chip cookies."

"What about a kiss instead?"

"One or six?" she teased, taking a tremulous breath.

"I'll start with one." He tried to keep the kiss teasing and gentle and light, but as soon as he tasted her, he wanted much more than a sample kiss. Christopher was napping upstairs, but Gillian was close by in the office.

Calling on all the restraint he possessed, he ended the kiss and lifted his head.

Sara smiled. "I guess I could give you a plate of cookies to share with Gillian."

"Ah, the bribery worked. Little do you know but my partner's leaving soon so I'll have them all to myself."

Sara poked him in the ribs. "I'll say good-bye before I go upstairs to wrap presents."

Jake raised the envelope he'd been holding in his hand. "I have something for you besides a kiss."

Sara glanced at the letterhead and took the envelope from him, sliding her finger under the flap and opening it. Withdrawing the sheet of paper, she unfolded it. "My final course schedule. Everything is set." With a quick grin, she said, "I'm really going back to school."

"You're excited about it."

"Yes. And grateful. I appreciate this opportunity, Jake. When I'm finished, I'll be able to teach and maybe make a difference."

He had no doubt she'd make a good teacher. But he couldn't help but wonder if she would have continued to work in a day care center or if she would have tried to follow her dream on her own if they hadn't gotten married. The doubts always snatched at his happiness.

"I'd better get back to Gillian. The sooner we go through that last batch of letters and e-mails, the sooner she'll get home." Jake left the kitchen, forgetting about the cookies.

Back in his office a few minutes later, he sank into his swivel chair.

"What happened?" Gillian asked.

"Nothing happened."

"You've been different lately. I thought maybe it was the season but my guess is your good mood has more to do with you and Sara. Except now, you left happy and came back sad."

"I'm trying to get my life in order and make a marriage with Sara. We're having our ups and downs. That's all."

"What's going on, Jake? I spend a lot of time in this office with you, and I think I know you. You're fighting some kind of battle and you won't let anyone help."

"Nobody can help."

"Not even Sara?"

"Sara's a part of the battle. We're getting closer. Sometimes it feels right. Sometimes it's damned uncomfortable."

"What's uncomfortable?"

"What I feel when I'm with her. The things she stirs up."

"What things?"

He could get annoyed with Gillian for prying or he could think about her question. "Feelings. Memories. My father leaving. My mother taking her life."

"Your son."

"Yes, Davie. Christopher reminds me of him, yet he has Sara's smile and her enthusiasm for anything new."

"But you sound as if that hurts you instead of bringing you pleasure."

"It does. I don't know why. It just does. That's what's confusing as hell."

"And as lonely," Gillian offered softly.

"I'm used to being alone."

"Being alone and being lonely are two different things."

The phone rang, and Gillian picked it up. From the quality of her smile, Jake knew who was on the other end before she covered the mouthpiece and said, "It's Nathan."

To her husband, she explained, "We have a stack of emails to go through yet. And I'd like to get some of the names into the computer."

Jake picked up the phone on his desk. "She'll be home as soon as she can. It's Christmas Eve and she should be with you and Matthew. Hang up your stocking, Bradley. Maybe Santa will come up with that Italian sports car you've had your eye on." Jake hung up the phone.

Gillian laughed. "Nathan? I guess Jake's saying he'll finish up here. I'll leave now. And when I get home, we'll talk about this item you must have asked Santa about but forgot to mention to me." She laughed again at something her husband said, tenderly murmured "I love you," and hung up. Then she grinned at Jake. "He said he'll get you later."

Sara appeared in the doorway to the office with a plate of cookies and put them on her husband's desk. "Gillian, I wanted to wish you a merry Christmas before I go upstairs."

"Merry Christmas to you, too. Do you have plans for tomorrow evening?" Gillian asked.

Jake chuckled. "Just playing with Christopher's toys."

"Then, why don't you come over? Mom's cooking up a storm. Nathan's girls will be there, too."

Jake looked at Sara and saw from her expression that she'd like to go. "Around six?"

Gillian took her purse from the bottom desk drawer. "Six is good." Coming out from behind the desk, she gave Jake a hug. "I hope Santa brings you everything you wish for." Releasing Jake, she went to Sara and gave her a hug. "And you, too."

Sara said to Jake, "I'll see Gillian to the door."

As the two women walked through the living room, Sara offered, "I'll bring along fudge I made if that's okay."

"If you have any left."

"I made two batches. Christopher and Jake don't know about the second one."

Gillian laughed. "Bring your aunt along if she'd like to come."

"I'm sure she will. She's coming for dinner and probably will stay through the afternoon." Sara opened the door for Gillian. "I want to thank you for your friendship. It means more than you know."

"You're an easy person to be friends with. Have a wonderful Christmas Eve. I'll see you tomorrow."

Sara closed the door. Tonight would be wonderful if she had anything to say about it—a festive dinner, hanging their stockings, reading Christopher holiday stories. Then after their son went to bed, maybe she and Jake could exchange their presents...then fall asleep in each other's arms.

Jake was typing information into the computer when his fax machine beeped. One piece of paper hummed out, then a second and a third. He swiveled toward the machine and lifted them out.

The first sheet was a letter from Sara's lawyer. Jake would have just collected the papers and taken them upstairs to Sara except one phrase caught his eye and the number on the line shocked him. The printed words jumped at him. Her lawyer urged her to accept the offer for her mother's land in Arizona, an offer for ten acres of land that spread over six digits!

As Jake read the letter, then looked over the contract, confusion rose in him. She'd said it was a little plot of land. Ten acres wasn't "little." Had she known about this offer? Had she known the property was worth this much? Had she lied to him again?

The figure blurred in front of his eyes. The turmoil inside him blinded him to gentler emotions that had been growing since his wedding day. The pain in his heart swelled until he rammed his fist on the desk. Damn her. Damn her for not telling him the truth. She'd said her parents had bought a little plot of land that was in the middle of nowhere...that might not ever sell!

With his hand closed on the papers, he mounted the steps slowly, dreading facing Sara, yet knowing he had no choice. Fleetingly, he thought about waiting to confront her, playing out Christmas Eve as if nothing had happened. But he wasn't an actor and he could never hide the betrayal he was feeling. Besides, Sara only had forty-eight hours to decide if she'd accept the offer. Why wouldn't she? Unless she knew the property could possibly bring in even more!

In his soul, he knew why she'd kept the truth from him, but he wanted to hear her say it.

Sara sat on Jake's bed, Christmas wrapping paper and bows scattered around her. She folded the paper on one end of a box and secured it with tape. As she looked up, she smiled.

But her smile faded when she saw his expression. "What's wrong?"

"Nothing's wrong. At least not for you. You're sitting pretty. Your lawyer just faxed you an offer on that plot of land in Arizona. Some 'little' plot." Jake dropped the papers on the bed.

Picking them up, she skimmed the letter. "Oh-my-gosh! I never expected anything like this."

"Drop the act, Sara."

Her chin came up. "Excuse me?"

"You can cut the surprise. *A little plot of land*, you said. *Might never sell*, you said. Some little plot of land. Did you expect me to not find out about it? I guess I never mentioned I told your lawyer he could use my fax number to send paperwork to you. If I hadn't made the offer, maybe I wouldn't have found out."

"Just what are you accusing me of?" Her voice had risen to match his.

"I'm accusing you of deceit. Again. You're getting good at it, Sara. Sorry I interfered."

"You're not making sense, Jake. I didn't know the land was worth this. I thought Mom and Dad had bought it almost like a dream to believe in."

"It's ten acres, Sara. That's no 'little' plot of land."

"I didn't know it was ten acres. Don't you understand? I never knew exactly what it was."

"You expect me to believe that?"

"Why shouldn't you?"

"Because you lied to me before," he almost shouted, the pain of losing her the first time still raw, the pain of losing his wife and son hitting him in the gut, the pain of missing Christopher's first three years hurting so badly he didn't think he'd ever forget it.

"Oh, Jake. I thought you were beginning to forgive me. But you haven't even started. Why would I lie to you? Why would I keep this from you no matter how much it was worth?"

The sadness on her face seemed real. Yet... "You came to me with no job and practically nothing. You needed help."

Her back straightened and she held her head high. "I did not need help. I came to you so you could get to know your son...and...and because I still loved you."

How he wished he could believe that. His childhood experiences, his cynicism as a cop, his doubts about

Sara's motives told him otherwise. "No. You knew if you had nothing, I'd take pity on you. I'd want to provide for you and our son."

"Pity? That's why you married me?" She seemed shocked.

He could deny it. He could tell her... What? That memories of what they'd had had played into the decision? That he'd started to trust her again but now all the doubts were back and maybe pity was all that was left? He wanted to escape his pain and some of it was landing on her. All he could do was tell her the truth. "I wanted to be near my son. You knew I'd jump on that chance after losing Davie. Marriage seemed to be the best way to accomplish that."

He saw her quick intake of breath before she said, "If I had known that was the only reason—" Her words seemed to get tied up in her throat.

He knew the feeling.

But then she managed to say, "I wouldn't marry a man who only married me out of pity. And if I thought Christopher was the only reason you asked me, I would have said no. I thought we still had something left. I have more self-respect than to be part of a loveless marriage." Her voice had risen and she took a deep calming breath. "But you seem to think you know everything. So what was I going to do when you did find out how much the property was worth? As my husband, you would have found out eventually."

The answer was obvious to him and ready on his tongue. It had a bitter taste. "That property could have taken forever to sell. As your lawyer explains, this development company sees the potential in it. My guess is when the windfall came through, then you were going to divorce me. Community property, profits from that land... You'd no longer need me to finance your life, your education, or Christopher's for that matter."

"You are so wrong."

His hands balled into fists as he gave her the suspicions that had burdened him since she returned, the suspicions that now seemed justified because of her lawyer's letter. "Not from where I'm standing. You didn't tell me you were pregnant. It took you until Christopher was more than three years old to tell me I had a son. Why? You lose your job. Your mother, your only security in this world dies. You feel adrift. You know you'll get little money from her belongings, and you have nothing else except a valuable piece of land. The problem is—it's not valuable unless it sells, and you have no idea when that will be. So you come to me, to use me, until you and Christopher don't need me anymore. It's all so clear now."

She hopped up from the bed, her movement causing rolls of paper to tumble to the floor. "Clear? The only thing that's clear is how muddled your thinking is. The trouble is—I know better than to try and convince you otherwise because you're more stubborn than any mule!" Hurrying to the hallway, she headed for the stairs.

In a few quick strides, Jake snagged her arm. "Where are you going?"

"For a walk. To sort things out. To think about the real estate offer. To pray that when I come back, you'll be willing to listen to reason."

On that note, she pulled away and hurried down the steps. The front door slammed, the sound reverberating through the house.

Jake sought refuge in his office and stared out the window, feeling numb. He didn't know what to believe anymore. He couldn't think. He couldn't feel. He could only ache without knowing why. The sun moved toward the west, its rays fading from the office. Without its warmth, the December air coming through the window became cooler.

He glanced at his watch. Christopher was usually up by now, peeking into the kitchen to see what his mother was cooking, or slipping into Jake's office to see what he was doing. Concerned, Jake went upstairs and pushed open the door to Christopher's room.

His son wasn't in his bed. Or in any other part of the room. Jake looked from corner to corner, from toy box to bookshelves. No Christopher. Maybe he was in Sara's room. What used to be Sara's room.

Jake pushed open the door and stepped inside. It still looked like her room. Her mother's perfume bottles sat on the vanity. A book she'd started before their trip to Las Vegas lay on the nightstand. A pair of black espadrilles sat by the chair. Her wicker handbag hung by its handle on the closet doorknob. Most of her belongings were still in this room. He hadn't suggested she move everything over and she hadn't asked. A pang of regret stung a place on his heart that hurt already.

He checked his room next, both bathrooms, and still didn't find his son. Worried, he called Christopher's name over and over then rushed downstairs. He examined every room, every corner. The kitchen door stood open. He pushed the screen door and plunged onto the back porch calling, "Christopher," over and over again.

Slowing her stride, Sara tried to calm herself, tried to believe she and Jake still had a chance. Why was he so determined to believe the worst of her? Why couldn't he take her at her word?

She didn't have an answer when she returned to the front door, out of breath, and still hurting. Taking a few deep breaths, she opened the door and went in.

Jake rushed in from the kitchen. "Have you seen Christopher?"

"Christopher? No. Why would—? Where is he?" Her voice rose with the panic she saw on Jake's face.

"I don't know. I can't tell you to stay calm because I can't. God, Sara, what are we going to do? I've looked everywhere. I'm ready to call Gillian and the police. What if he wandered into the yard and somebody took him?"

Jake was the private investigator, the former cop who knew all about the dark side, about what could go wrong rather than right. She'd taught Christopher boundaries. He couldn't have broken through all of them. "Tell me what happened."

Jake paced across the living room. "I went upstairs to get him up, and he wasn't there."

"He doesn't take a nap everyday."

Jake stopped for a moment. "Of course, he does. We put him in his room—"

Shaking her head, she explained, "Some days he falls asleep. Others, he reads or plays."

After a tense pause, Jake mowed his hand through his hair. "All right. Maybe he wasn't napping. But he should still be in his room."

"Not if he heard us arguing. Not if he got scared."

The worry in Jake's brown eyes changed to panic again. "So we're back to where he would go. Honest to God, Sara..."

"Did you check all his hide-and-seek hiding places?"

"What are you talking about?"

"When we play hide and seek. When you two play in the yard he always hides behind the crepe myrtle or next to the shed or under the sliding board. He has hiding places in the house, too. We play while you're working."

"Where?" Jake was already heading for the stairs.

"Jake, if he's scared, I don't want to scare him more."

Jake stopped on the first step. "All right. I'm calm. Now show me."

Sara crossed to him and gave him a gentle push. "Look under your bed." His body tensed under her hands and she remembered every word of their disagreement. Then he climbed the steps, moving away from her touch and she sighed, telling herself to handle one crisis at a time.

Christopher wasn't under the bed or in the bathtub or behind his toy box. Sara went to the closet in her bedroom, Jake tight on her heels. Opening the door, she flicked on the light and almost collapsed from relief when she saw two small stockinged feet on the left side of the closet. She alerted Jake by pointing.

When he saw Christopher's feet, the relief on Jake's face was obvious. So was the love as he sat down on the floor.

Sara pushed her clothes aside and curled up next to their son, too. "Watcha doin'?"

"Nothin'."

"We couldn't find you. We were very worried."

Jake tapped Christopher's foot because the three-year-old was staring at his lap and wouldn't look up. "You shouldn't hide from us."

"You yelled at Mommy." His big brown eyes were shiny, and Sara could imagine what Christopher's accusing look was doing to Jake.

"And I yelled back," she added. "Christopher, your dad and I had an argument. Adults do that some times. We didn't mean to scare you."

"You did."

Sara slipped her arm around him, tucking him close to her side. "We're sorry. Especially today. Christmas Eve is special. We want you to be happy, not afraid."

"Are you and Daddy still mad?"

She couldn't speak for Jake, and she wouldn't lie to their son. "We have to talk some more before we know. But I'll tell you what. Your Dad and I will forget about being mad at each other until after Christmas. Christmas isn't a time for being mad. It's a time to give lots of love and hugs and kisses."

"And presents," Christopher added.

"And presents," Jake agreed, holding out his arms to his son. "C'mon, partner. Let's go get your sneakers. You and I can play ball while your mom gets supper ready."

Christopher moved from Sara's side and went willingly into Jake's arms. "Okay."

Jake's brown eyes met Sara's over Christopher's head. Nothing was settled, and the tension from their argument still vibrated between them. But they would both do whatever they could to make their son feel loved and secure.

Before Sara cleaned up the mess on Jake's bed, she called her lawyer to find out exactly what was going on with her mother's property. Expecting to get his answering machine or service, she was relieved when he answered himself.

"Just in the nick of time, Sara. My secretary left and I'm on my way out."

"I won't hold you up. I just wondered about the property in Arizona...what you think of the contract...why they offered so much. I thought this was just an undeveloped plot of land. I never knew it was ten acres. I never knew it was worth so much."

"Jennie and I didn't know it could be worth that, either. A few months ago, you might have gotten a quarter of that sum. But you lucked out. A highway is going to be cutting through that area. The developer who wants to buy your property is planning a shopping center. I'd advise you to take the offer, Sara. It won't get much better than that."

"I still can't believe it."

"Believe it. A highway can transform rural property into prime real estate. The fax was just to let you look over the paperwork. You'll have to come into my office day after tomorrow and sign the contract. If you have any questions, make a list. I'll answer them for you then. You have a Merry Christmas."

Sara wished him the same and said good-bye, not caring about the offer or the money. All she cared about was the way Jake perceived it.

As she prepared dinner, she peeked out the window and saw her husband and son playing ball. Jake rolled a ball across the grass. Christopher ran after it, picked it up in his pudgy little hands and tried to toss it back to Jake. The ball tossing turned into a game of tag and then as Jake stood by and watched, Christopher climbed up then slid down the sliding board.

When Sara called for them to wash up, Jake scooped up his son and put him on his shoulders until they got to the porch. She took the roast chicken out of the oven and had everything ready when Jake and Christopher came into the kitchen. Busyness held her fears at bay, at least for the time being.

The tension between her and Jake was palpable, but they talked with Christopher and kept conversation between themselves to a minimum. After dinner, they hung three stockings on the mantel. Finally, Christopher nestled between them on the sofa and Sara read the Christmas story.

"An angel talked to the shepherds," Christopher said when Sara closed the book.

Sara kissed him on the top of his head. "Angels help guide us. Tomorrow morning, you tell us if you heard the Christmas angel."

With a sleepy nod, he mumbled, "I will."

By the time they put milk and cookies on the mantel for Santa, Christopher was yawning. Jake carried him piggyback up the stairs. As any three-year-old on Christmas Eve, he prolonged his bedtime ritual. But by the time Sara and Jake kissed him goodnight, he was hugging his teddy bear and his eyes closed in slumber.

Sara went downstairs, going over in her mind what she could say to Jake, how she could make him believe her. She'd taken a bag of small presents from the foyer closet and was placing them in Christopher's stocking when Jake came downstairs. His expression was serious, and Sara didn't know what was going to happen next.

"Would you like something to drink?" he asked. "I'm going to get a brandy."

"No, thanks."

Jake unlocked the top of a bookcase. Inside, stood a shelf of glasses and a few bottles of liquor. Sara didn't even know that was there. She'd never looked inside. Jake poured a small amount into a snifter and closed the cabinet. "It's my fault he got scared. What if he had found his way downstairs and out the door?"

She should have realized Jake would take responsibility for upsetting Christopher. "He knows the rules, Jake. He's never supposed to go outside alone."

Jake swirled the amber liquid in his glass. "When he's afraid, he might forget the rules. I just want to keep him safe, Sara. How can I do that?"

She couldn't keep away from Jake, she couldn't keep from standing close and wanting to erase the anguish from his eyes. "We will keep him safe. We'll tell him everything he should know for his own good, and we'll protect him every way we can. But we can't lock him in a cocoon away from the real world."

Jake downed the brandy in two swallows, set the glass on the shelf, then held her by her shoulders. "Why can't we? Why can't we just keep him in here with us so we know he's safe?"

She searched his eyes, seeing the sadness and doubts, the fear and the pain. "Because that's not letting him live."

"Dammit, Sara. Look how easy it would be to lose him. It could have happened today."

He was thinking of Christopher, but he was thinking of Davie, too. "Don't do this to yourself, Jake."

"You can say that now. But how forgiving would you be if Christopher had wandered outside? If something had happened?"

She closed her eyes and tried to imagine it. She couldn't. It was too painful. So she could only guess the pain and guilt that Jake felt about Davie. Reaching out, she stroked his jaw. "You've got to let it go, Jake. Please, try to let it go."

She didn't know if he was trying to block out memories or create new ones when he kissed her. All she knew was that he was kissing her as if he needed her forever. There was a fever in the kiss and a desperation that made her heart trip. And something about it brought tears to her eyes.

The first kiss caught fire and gave birth to another...and another. The first touch led to another...and another. There were no more firsts between them as the sparks flew and their passion exploded. The brandy on

Jake's tongue became intoxicating. He removed her jogging suit in the same amount of time it took for her to tug off his T-shirt and unsnap his jeans. Their clothes fell away as they tried to kiss more, touch more, feel more.

Jake's beard stubble rasped across her breast. Her nails scraped his back. As he took her down to the carpet, she wrapped her arms around his waist. When she lay back, he came with her. Bracing his arms on either side of her, he thrust into her with an anguished groan. Suddenly, she knew why tears had filled her eyes earlier and why they were filling them now. He wanted her, maybe he even needed her, but he was afraid to love her. She might never know his love. She might never know all of Jake.

In desperation, she gave herself to him. She kissed him and held him tight, trying to show him just how much she wanted, needed, and loved him. Giving herself up to him, she let him give her pleasure, climbed higher and higher with him, until they climaxed together, holding on to each other as if they'd never let go.

But a few moments later, Jake did let go. He slid to his side and said like a judge pronouncing a sentence, "We didn't use protection."

Chapter Ten

Jake's accusations that Sara had kept the value of the property from him had hurt, but his doubts about the birth control actually felt as if they cracked her heart. When he'd made love to her just now without additional protection, she'd thought maybe they had a chance. She'd thought maybe it was a conscious decision on his part to show her he could trust her. But apparently passion had driven him, had driven them both and it had had nothing to do with trust at all.

"I told you before, I'm on the pill."

His silence was his response.

All the weeks of patience Sara had cultivated, all the loving thoughts she'd nurtured about time healing, and time proving how much she loved Jake lit a fuse leading directly to anger. Jake had been the angry one. She had deserved some of it. But she didn't deserve his constant lack of trust, and now she was angry, angrier than she'd ever been.

The surge of it almost left her breathless. "You're never going to believe I love you, are you?"

His voice was cold. "You told me you loved me four years ago then you called off the wedding."

They were back to that again. There was something else she wasn't seeing, something that went much deeper than leaving him at the altar. But right now the disappointment and hurt sending adrenaline through her wouldn't give her the time to think it through.

"I loved you enough not to trap you, Jake."

He looked startled. She had never put it in those terms before. "You're so sure I would have seen it as a trap?"

"Yes. You see in black and white, good or bad. There's no gray, nor room for human imperfections. I made a mistake—a giant one, I'll grant you. I loved you so much I didn't want to go into a marriage with you resenting me or a child you didn't want. I was thinking about all of us. But then I realized what a terrible mistake I'd made, and I told you about Christopher. You want to give me every kind of motive except for the one that counted—I still loved you. But you can't believe that. You'd rather think I want a free ride, that I'm biding my time until I have enough money to leave again. Get real, Jake. What happens to my emotions and Christopher's in all that? Do you think I'd put him through it?"

Deep creases lined Jake's forehead. "It's hard to believe you knew nothing about the value—"

"Jake, wake up! All I knew was that my parents had bought a plot of land. It was the only thing they'd ever owned. After Dad died, it was Mom's little bit of security. Mr. Gunthry says the price is up now because a highway will run through the area."

Her words didn't seem to move Jake. He was still silent.

She shook her head as tears came to her eyes. "You know, I used to think you were a kind, compassionate man who'd seen the worst part of life, but still tried to make it better for others. But with me, you're so hard and cold sometimes. It's ironic. You reunite people but you won't open your heart to reunite us. You don't trust me enough to let me get within ten yards, except when we make love and even then you hold back. Do you think I can't tell? Do you know how it hurts that you don't trust me enough to let me know all of you?"

He sat up and stared straight ahead. "Don't you know how it hurts me that I can't trust you?"

Sara's dreams withered. At the words that were so harsh now that they were out in the open, she knew what she had to say and what she had to do for all their sakes. "Jake, there's nothing I can do to prove I loved you then, and I love you now. You have to either believe me or not. That's up to you. I'm tired of trying to prove it. I'm tired of trying to earn your love, seek your approval, do and say the right thing so you don't distrust me more. Don't you think Christopher can feel the tension between us?"

"This afternoon won't happen again."

She stared at his profile, loving him, but hurting too much to keep her feelings inside. "What will we do next time? Make sure the door's closed? A misunderstanding doesn't stay behind a closed door, neither does a lack of trust. The tension's not good for Christopher. It's not good for us. I can't live with you any more, loving you but knowing you don't love me. I thought we could get back what we had, but I was wrong, so very wrong. We'll stay here through tomorrow, but then Christopher and I will go back to Aunt El's until I find a place of our own. I'll let you see Christopher whenever you want. You're his father, and I'll never interfere in your relationship with him."

Jake turned toward her then, his face hard, his jaw set until he said in a steel-edged voice, "If you leave, I'll sue for custody."

Sara didn't think the pain in her heart could get any worse, but she was wrong. "Do you want to trap me, Jake? Do you want to trap Christopher in an untenable situation? Don't you understand yet that love can't survive under those conditions? That's why I wouldn't trap you!"

His silence brought more tears to her eyes and sobs to her throat. She couldn't stand the coldness any longer. He was keeping all barriers in place, and she just didn't have the strength to knock them down, especially when she knew he wouldn't let her. She dressed faster than she'd ever dressed in her life. All she wanted to do was escape to her room so he couldn't see the extent of her devastation.

He gave no sign that he even saw her leave. She climbed the steps feeling as if Christmas would never come again.

The chill of the room didn't affect Jake as much as the chill around his heart. He felt cold inside, so cold, like he'd never be warm again. He glanced at the steps. The hall light was out.

Dressing mechanically, he checked his pocket for his car keys, and then he headed for the garage. There was someplace he had to go, someplace he went every holiday and many days in between. Except...he'd missed this Thanksgiving. He hadn't been there since Sara had arrived.

This late on Christmas Eve, there wasn't much traffic. Most people were home with their families. He turned into the cemetery with a sense of relief, a sense of the familiar. A few minutes later, he stood in front of the plaque with his son's name.

"Davie, how I wish you could talk to me. I wish you could let me feel you."

Silence. An absence of feeling. Numbness.

In trying to protect himself from getting hurt again, had he become numb to everything?

Yes.

"Davie?"

Jake felt emotion welling up inside of him and didn't try to suffocate it. He let it rise as uncomfortable and painful as it was. His heart raced, his chest tightened, and he felt tears prick his eyes. Damn, it hurt. It hurt so much...

"Why did you leave, Davie? Why did our father leave, and Mom and Mary Beth? Why does everyone I love leave?"

The strength of the pain, the ache around Jake's heart, brought him to the ground. On his knees, he stared at his son's name and prayed for deliverance from the hurt, the loneliness, the emptiness. The chill of night swirled around him, the silence echoed his question over and over.

After a while the echo stopped.

Sara is leaving, too.

"I knew she wouldn't stay."

You knew?

"She left before. She didn't love me enough..."

She loved you too much.

Too much.

Was it as simple as that? Had Sara's love been so pure and true she couldn't stand to see it compromised? And when she'd tried to love him again... He'd thrown it back in her face. No wonder she wanted to leave.

What had he done?

She'd said she couldn't stand to live with him knowing he didn't love her. But that wasn't true. He did love her. He'd loved her since he met her. But now it was too late. His father, mother, Davie and Mary Beth had left. He could do nothing to prevent their leaving. But Sara...

Tell her you love her.

Was that enough? What had she said—she couldn't prove to him that she loved him. But she had proved it, over and over again, with every act, every word, every touch. Could he undo the damage? Was trust simply a conscious decision?

No, it's a leap of faith.

"Davie, Davie, are you here?"

Silence answered Jake again, but a comforting sense of peace wound about him. He suddenly knew that he could do nothing about the past, but he was responsible for his future. Ungodly things happened, but that didn't mean there wasn't a God. Black wasn't always black, and white wasn't always white. Shades of both reflected the world in which he lived.

He felt shaken...different...changed. Changed in his heart and soul. But he was certain of one thing. He loved Sara, and love was something he couldn't turn his back on, not anymore. He needed her love. He'd just been too afraid to accept it. Now somehow he had to convince her that love was the wonderful gift she thought it was. He had to convince her he was worth another try.

As Jake rose to his feet, one star shined brighter than all the rest.

The garage door opening alerted Sara that Jake was leaving. She had no idea where he was going. Tears still lingered too near the surface for her to brush them away, for her to brush the hurt away. Had she really told Jake she was leaving? Wouldn't that be the best thing for everyone?

She uncurled her legs, pushed herself out of her bedroom chair, and went to stand in the doorway to Christopher's room. He slept so peacefully, so innocently. Suddenly she remembered his presents. She had to put them under the tree.

It took her three trips, and once she'd arranged them to her satisfaction, tears blurred her eyes all over again. Wrapping her arms around herself, she went to the kitchen to make a cup of tea. Through the kitchen window, she could see one star shining brighter than all the others. She opened the door and stepped out onto the porch.

With her hands on the balustrade, she gazed up at the bright white light. She loved Jake. As sure as the star was shining, she'd never stop.

So why are you leaving? The voice seemed to come from deep inside her.

"I can't keep battling his defenses. I can't keep trying to prove I love him."

Why not just love him?

The simplicity of the question stunned her. Was that the problem? That she was trying to prove something instead of loving him? Could he sense that? Was she on guard, too?

She tried to remember what he'd said earlier. He'd said she'd called off the wedding. He'd sounded so hurt, so...abandoned. Jake had been abandoned over and over again. By his father, his mother, and in a way his son and wife, too. Then Sara had left before their wedding. Did he expect the people he loved to leave him? Is that why he protected himself so?

Of course. Why hadn't she seen it before?

Because she was as caught up in the present situation as he was. They'd been so busy guarding themselves, trying to make the marriage work....

If she left now, she'd prove to him again that the people he loved deserted him.

But did he love her?

She thought about the birthday party he'd given her, his possessiveness, his support of her decision to go back to school, his passion and tenderness when he made love to her. He might not admit it, but he loved her. Jake wasn't a man to pretend anything.

So, what are you going to do?

She wouldn't leave. Like water on stone, she'd wear him down until he admitted what he felt. She'd do it by being herself and loving him. Tonight, her anger and disappointment had gotten the best of her. Maybe tomorrow morning, in the light of day, he'd listen to her. And if he didn't...

She heard the garage door open and close, and she held her breath.

First, Jake went up to Sara's room. This afternoon when the front door had slammed, he'd known she'd be back. But tonight, with the quiet click of the guest room door, he'd realized she'd never put her heart in his hands again. But maybe he could change that. Maybe...

When he found her room empty, he almost panicked. But with a quick look into Christopher's room, seeing his son sleeping, he knew she hadn't gone very far. Returning to the downstairs, he saw the dim glare of light from the kitchen. He'd missed it when he came in in his rush to see her.

The back door stood open and, with his heart thumping madly in his ears, he stepped outside. She was looking up at the sky, toward the brightest star, as if seeking guidance. He could use some of that himself.

"Sara?"

She turned, but her face was shadowed. He didn't know if she'd let him touch her, but he was beyond caring about logic or good sense. He took her hands in his. They were cold. He wanted to give her all the heat inside him, everything he could.

So he plunged in, praying she wouldn't shut him out the way he had her, praying she'd listen. "I know you've made a decision, and you think it's for the best. But you're wrong." When her hands fluttered in his, he rushed on. "I've been an idiot. I was so afraid of letting myself love you, so afraid that you'd leave again, I've been driving you away. I don't have any excuse. I don't know what to say to make things right—"

"I've changed my mind about leaving," she interrupted in a quiet, gentle voice. "I love you, Jake. And someday you're going to wake up and see it. I'm going to talk to you about it, and touch you, and just simply love you until you let down some of those walls and let me in. If necessary, maybe we'll have to see a counselor..."

He saw the worried look on her face, the concern that he'd argue with her, reject her again. But he saw the determination, too, and his heart swelled with even more love for her. "Everything you said today was true. I have been shutting you out. I don't want to do that ever again. Because I love you, Sara. And I don't want to lose you. I want you to help me see the shades between black and white and all the colors, too."

"You...love me?" She sounded breathless, as if she couldn't believe he was saying it.

"More than I ever thought possible. Since you and Christopher came into my life, I've felt the stirrings of happiness again." Looking deep into her eyes to make sure she understood, he went on, "I can trust you now because I've finally realized what a sacrifice you made four years ago. You put my needs before yours. Now I'm going to put your needs first for the rest of our lives. I didn't distrust you, Sara, as much as I didn't trust myself—to feel again...to love again. Can you forgive me? Can we start over?"

Tears ran down her cheeks. "I don't want to start over. I want to remember everything we've shared and go on from here."

He took her face between his palms and tenderly brushed the tears from her cheeks with his thumbs. "I've hurt you. I never meant to hurt you. I was so damn busy trying to protect myself..."

"Let's both forgive the hurt and concentrate on the love."

He encircled her with his arms and brought her closer. "I do love you, Sara. I'll spend every day for the rest of my life proving it."

"You don't have to prove anything. Just love me."

His lips found hers and made promises he knew he'd keep for a lifetime. Sara promised back, lacing her hands in his hair, loving him.

Suddenly, a sound wound around them. Music? No. Chimes.

They both lifted their heads at the same time.

The chimes on the Christmas angel were moving gently against each other.

Sara's eyes rounded, then she smiled. "I guess Santa arrived."

Jake touched his finger to his tongue and held it up in the air. "Sara, there's no wind."

She laughed—a sound as sweet as the chimes. "No, there isn't. On Christmas Eve, there's magic...and miracles."

Jake pointed to the bright star. "That guided me home. And while it was guiding me..." He squeezed her closer. "I thought about what I'd say to you. I thought a lot about my life, about Davie and Christopher. About us. I realized what a gift children are. And I thought that maybe in a year or so, we could have another child, so Christopher can learn all about sharing first-hand."

"Jake, are you sure?" The question was a gasp of surprise.

He understood her astonishment, the idea had stunned him as well. But he'd thought about it on the drive home. "Yes, I'm sure. And although Christopher needs a brother or sister, there's another more important reason I want to have another child—to show how much I love you."

Resting her hands on his shoulders, Sara said with certainty, "You can do that without us making a baby."

"I know. But I don't want any barriers, Sara. I want your heart to flow into mine and mine to flow into yours. I want it all."

She wound her arms around him and laid her cheek against his heart. "This truly is a night for miracles."

Jake held Sara tight against him and gazed at the star. A night for miracles...Christmas Eve, and he was so thankful he was holding his Christmas angel in his arms.

Epilogue

One Year Later

A bottle of champagne stood chilling on the nightstand beside the bed. Jake had fixed a tray of cheese and crackers while Sara showered. He'd bought a special present for her this Christmas, and he preferred giving it to her in their bed.

The bathroom door opened and Sara emerged, a white satin nightgown flowing with her as she came toward him. Jake swallowed hard. His pulse hammered, and as always when he saw her, his heart overflowed with love.

"You're breathtaking—my Christmas angel."

She arched her brows. "I'm no angel and we both know it."

As she slid into the other side of the bed, he chuckled. "No, you're a lovely woman who's as stubborn as I am sometimes."

Smiling knowingly, she gestured to the food and champagne. "What's all this?"

"I thought we should celebrate. In my heart, Christmas Eve is really our anniversary. I guess I never told you everything that happened that night. We've been so happy, I didn't want to bring up anything to remind you of the rough times."

Sara sidled closer to him and laid her hand on his chest. "Don't you know by now you can tell me anything?"

Over the past year, he'd confided in her many times about hopes and fears, and dreams for their future. "I know. And I guess that's why I thought about this tonight. Why I want to tell you."

Curling up beside him with her head on his shoulder, she urged, "So tell me."

He loved her there, beside him, always. "I told you I went to the cemetery last Christmas Eve and that the brightest star gave me hope and guided me back to you. What I didn't tell you was that I actually thought I heard a voice pointing my thinking in the right direction."

She popped up and looked into his eyes. "I did, too! When I was gazing at the star." She thought about it for a moment. "Do you think it was Davie, or for me—my mother?"

"Maybe. Or the same Christmas angel who touched the chimes. I don't know. But I do know I want to remember that night forever because I realized I had to let go of the past so I could believe in our love for the future. I thought you might want to remember it, too." He took a small box from between the pillows and set it in her lap. "Merry Christmas."

Her eyes glistened with tears.

"Don't cry yet. Open it first," he teased.

She tore off the bow and unwrapped the box. When she opened it, she gasped. A solitaire diamond surrounded by smaller ones twinkled up at her. "The star!"

She'd guessed without him telling her. "Do you like it?"

"It's beautiful. Will you put it on for me?"

He took the ring from the box and slid it onto her finger above the wedding band. "The jeweler said women wear rings like that with their bands. But if you think it's too much, you can wear it on your other hand."

She leaned over and gave him a kiss that told him it wasn't too much, it was just right. When he drew her on top of him so he could show her how much he loved her, she resisted and leaned away.

"What's wrong?"

She smiled and smoothed her hand over his brow. "Nothing. Except I want to give you your gift, too. It's just not quite as tangible...yet."

"I don't understand."

"Well, I can munch on the cheese and crackers over there, but I can't have any champagne."

He saw the glow on her face, the new lushness to her body he thought came from being happily married, and he knew. "You're pregnant!"

She nodded. "The doctor confirmed it yesterday. Are you...pleased?"

They'd talked about having another child many times, but had decided to let it happen naturally without giving the matter undue attention. "Yes, I'm pleased. I'm more than pleased." With a resounding kiss, he told her exactly how pleased. This time when he drew her on top of him, she didn't resist.

He broke the kiss only to murmur, "Merry Christmas, Mrs. Donovan."

Tracing her fingers over his lips, she smiled. "Merry Christmas, Mr. Donovan."

Jake reached to the nightstand and switched off the light.

But the room still glowed with their love. As Jake told Sara again with words and kisses and touches how much he loved her, one brilliant star twinkled at them through the window. In the distance, chimes played delicately, yet no wind blew.

Because it was Christmas Eve—a night for love, magic and miracles.

KAREN ROSE SMITH BOOKS
AVAILABLE IN E-BOOK FORMAT

FINDING MR. RIGHT Series
Kit and Kisses, Book 1 *
Forever After, Book 2 *
When Mom Meets Dad, Book 3 *
Falling For Her Boss, Book 4 *
Toys and Baby Wishes, Book 5 *
Love in Bloom, Book 6
Ribbons and Rainbows, Book 7 *
Wish on the Moon, Book 8 *
A Man Worth Loving, Book 9 *

SEARCH FOR LOVE Series
Nathan's Vow, Book 1 *
Jake's Bride, Book 2 *
Always Devoted, Book 3 *
Always Her Cowboy, Book 4 *
Heartfire, Book 5
Cassidy's Cowboy, Book 6 *
Her Sister, Book 7 *

FOREVER LOVE Series
April's Promise, Book 1 *

EVERYDAY LOVE Short Story Series
Everyday Cinderellas, Vol. 1
Everyday Prince Charming, Vol. 2
Everyday Romance, Vol.3

Garden of Fantasy
Abigail and Mistletoe
Writing is a Business

SCIENCE FICTION
SHORT STORY COLLECTION
Journey Into Chaos

BOXED SETS
Finding Mr. Right Boxed Set One
Finding Mr. Right Boxed Set Two
Search For Love Boxed Set One
Search For Love Boxed Set Two
Everyday Love Boxed Set

* Also available in audio book format

Excerpt from ALWAYS DEVOTED
Search For Love series, Book 3

Chapter One

"What do you believe happened to your sister?"

Emma Henderson felt her throat tighten and she found swallowing difficult. She hated the glare of the television lights and found her gaze swinging away from the camera to offstage where Linc Granger stood. The successful TV producer, who garnered high ratings with his specials, had convinced her this interview might help find Paige. That was the only reason she'd agreed to do it.

"I don't know what happened to Paige, Ms. Kahill. She left one afternoon to drive to San Francisco for the weekend and I haven't seen her since." Emma's voice cracked.

She almost felt Linc Granger take a step forward. To do what? Stop the interview with journalist, Tessa Kahill? To comfort her? To tell her everything was going to be okay when she knew it wasn't?

"Her car was found on the shoulder of the highway and she was missing. Can you tell me what your thoughts were when you found out?" the world-renown journalist asked.

"I was stunned. I couldn't believe it. At first we all thought she might have been kidnapped. But there was no call...no note for ransom...nothing."

"You were on the police list of persons of interest for a while, weren't you?"

"Tessa!" Linc Granger's deep voice rent the air with authority. He told the technicians to cut and take five. Then he strode up beside the interviewer.

His gaze connected to Emma's for a heart-stopping moment.

She tore her eyes from his and took a deep breath. She shouldn't have this reaction to him. He'd been compassionate toward her, protective even, and she was grateful. That's all there was to it.

But as Linc and the beautiful, curly-haired interviewer argued over the questions for the remainder of the interview to be aired later in the week, Emma knew she felt a spark of something with Linc Granger she'd never felt with her late husband Barrett.

After another minute or two of discussion, Linc crossed over to her chair and towered over her. He raked his hand through his dark brown hair, his green eyes turbulent. "Tessa insists she has to go this route. She thinks it's better if everything is out there in the public's face. I don't necessarily agree. I know you lost your husband a year ago and this is hard. If you'd rather Tessa go in a different direction—"

As Emma shook her head, her honey-blond hair fell over her shoulder. "The family is always questioned. The family is always of interest. It's okay, Mr. Granger."

"It's Linc," he said gently. As cutting as his voice had been a few moments before, it was so different now.

Ever since their first meeting, she'd felt strangely out of breath. She was a mother with a four-year-old, and her sister was missing. She couldn't think about anything else.

Squaring her shoulders, she assured him, "I can handle Ms. Kahill's questions."

As Linc Granger studied her, she felt almost all of the air get sucked out of the room. What was it about him that made her so flustered? He was older, between thirty-five and forty she guessed, and she felt young at twenty-six for the first time in years. She'd taken on a lot of responsibility early.

After a few moments, he reassured her again. "If anything makes you too uncomfortable, you can say so. I'm sorry I wasn't here when the interview started. I would have laid down some ground rules." He glared at Tessa as she was studying her notes.

"When you offered me the opportunity to publicize Paige's disappearance again, you said Tessa Kahill was the best. Maybe you should let her do her job. Before we started, she told me she has to be on a plane out of L.A. tonight to Afghanistan."

"You like her," Linc noted with a wry smile.

"We talked before the interview. Yes, I do. And I respect her."

"Good." He sounded relieved. "Then I'll let her continue and I won't interfere again. But I would like to discuss something with you when this is over. Do you have time?"

What could he want to discuss with her? They'd spoken at length about what had happened to Paige, the little bit she knew, and Emma's desire to stay out of the spotlight for her daughter's sake. But he seemed to have something important to say and she did want to hear it.

"My next door neighbor is watching Becky. I'll have some time."

He was quiet for a few moments, but the intensity of his expression suddenly gave her the knowledge that Linc Granger was a very different man than Barrett Henderson had been.

It shouldn't matter.

But she found herself wanting to listen to Linc, even though she suspected that simple conversation with him could unsettle her life even more.

What a stupid thing to do!

Linc never interrupted the flow of an interview. When he'd asked Tessa to do this, she'd told him she could fit it in during a layover in L.A. She'd been in Mexico interviewing some diplomat, and then she was gone again for Afghanistan to tape a special report.

So why had he jumped in?

Because Emma Trent Henderson fascinated him. She and her four-year-old daughter had been through the cable news wringer when her sister had disappeared three months ago. Yet she'd somehow retained her dignity and poise. Still, the lost look in her expressive brown eyes when she spoke about her sister, Paige, haunted him.

From her first press conference, he'd been intrigued by her and her story. Maybe because he knew someone who could help her if she wanted to be helped. Unorthodox means weren't for everyone, but he had the feeling Emma had exhausted the usual channels.

The cameras were rolling again and Tessa was asking more questions. As he listened to the rest of the interview, he became more sure about the information he wanted to give Emma. When he heard Tessa end her questions with, "Tell me how you feel as a widow, with a four-year-old to raise and no idea where your sister is," he listened hard.

Emma didn't hesitate to say softly, "Sometimes I feel as if I'm in limbo. I'm searching for answers and I don't know if I'll ever find them."

Linc knew he had to tell Emma about Gillian Bradley and her special gift.

When Emma finished the interview, she felt wrung out. Not a new feeling these days. But after she thanked Tessa, she turned to find Linc waiting for her. It was easy for her to think of using his first name and she wasn't sure exactly why.

She'd worn a flowered sundress for the interview, a dress she often wore when taking sales orders in her gift basket shop, *Occasional Baskets*. But now she wished she'd worn something a little more sophisticated...because Linc Granger in his custom-tailored suit, tie and expensive shirt shouted sophistication.

Who was she kidding?

She'd never been sophisticated. Hard working and tasteful, maybe, but never sophisticated.

After the camera lights shut down and she stood, Linc took her elbow. She felt the heat from his fingers through her whole body. It was an odd, wake-up feeling that she'd never experienced with Barrett.

Barrett. He'd only been gone a year. How could she even be attracted to someone else?

Okay, so that's what this feeling was toward Linc Granger...attraction. So much for that. He certainly didn't drive his car in her neighborhood.

Linc glanced around the set where techs were bustling by and men in suits strode purposefully here and there. He frowned.

Even frowning, his face was ruggedly handsome with character lines around his eyes that cut deep. From laughter? Or worry?

Turning his focus back to her, he asked, "My car service picked you up, right?"

"Yes, thank you. It was nice to relax for a change driving into the city."

He smiled, and then the smile slipped away. He actually looked uncertain for a moment, but only for a very fleeting moment. "We're not going to find privacy here," he explained. "Even in my office I'm constantly interrupted. Would you consider taking a drive? I have a place on the beach—"

At her surprised expression he held up his hand in a "stop" gesture. "This is not a proposition," he assured her, his voice lowering. "I can even provide you numbers of a few good friends if you want to check me out. I just believe we need privacy for this discussion."

And just what discussion was it? "I checked you out before I agreed to do this interview," she admitted. "At least as much as I could."

He looked mildly amused. "So, what did you find when you checked me out?"

"I found out that everything you do pretty much turns to gold. You went to Cal State for a degree in Cinema and TV Arts. You directed a couple of small films, afterward turning that money over into investments. Then you started gathering professionals around you who wanted to make the same films and then TV shows that you did. You've produced cable documentaries as well as network hits. But that all involves business, not your character or your personal life."

"My personal life is off limits to reporters." That was said without any amusement at all.

"I did find a couple of Google images with you escorting celebrities or models to charity functions and social galas. But that really didn't tell me much."

His eyebrows arched, thick eyebrows over deep green eyes that made her feel a little fluttery inside. Okay, maybe a lot fluttery inside.

"So why did you decide to do the interview?" he asked.

"Because I found transcripts of other interviews you produced. They were honest and considerate of whomever was being interviewed. I also liked your..." She hesitated. "Your point of view when we talked. I didn't feel you were going to sensationalize what had happened to me. You proved it just now when you stepped in."

The nerve in his almost-square jaw worked for a moment. Then that small giveaway of tension was gone. "I want to discuss something other than letting the police direct the investigation to find your sister."

That's all she needed to hear. "Let's go for that drive."

A half-hour later they were in Linc's sporty silver luxury sedan, heading toward the ocean. Up until now they'd made small talk about the interview, about Tessa, about Emma's daughter who was learning so fast and growing so much. She'd called Becky's sitter before they'd left to make sure Maris and her daughter could find something for supper if she wasn't back in time.

At a lull in the conversation, Emma watched Linc's large hands on the steering wheel. He'd discarded his suit jacket and tie and opened the top two buttons on his shirt before he'd climbed into the car. Sitting beside him like this, the atmosphere seemed oddly intimate as the day started winding down and the sun sank lower on the horizon.

"Not much longer," he told her.

She sent him a small smile. "Am I looking impatient?"

"No, just a little nervous. Are you sure you don't want to call my best friend?"

That probably would have been wise. But Linc seemed straightforward. "Tell me about your best friend."

After Linc cut her a glance, he focused on the highway again. "His name is Nathan Bradley. He's a family man with two daughters from his first marriage he sees a lot, and a little boy, Matthew, from his second marriage.

He's an internet security expert who flies all over the country, taking care of important people's networks."

"I like the fact that you put his family history before his work."

"Would it make you feel better if I told you I baby-sit for Nathan? I did before he married Gillian and I do now. Their kids call me Uncle Linc."

She laughed. "Maybe I should talk to *them*."

He laughed, too, and glanced at her again. Something intangible passed between them that she seemed to feel in her heart. How crazy was that?

Fifteen minutes later, Linc turned off the highway and took a series of turns. After he drove down a long drive, they exited the car and Emma looked around.

A one-story house sprawled before her and she could see the ocean beyond. "What a beautiful setting," she murmured.

"I like it. It's worth the commute. We're alone here. If you prefer to walk the beach instead of going inside, I'll understand."

Alone with Linc Granger. Maybe she should have trepidations about that, but she didn't. She felt excited. Because they were going to talk about a way to find her sister? Or because he was one very sexy man?

Because he was going to give her information to find a way to find Paige, of course.

"I'll shed my shoes and we can walk the beach," she decided, taking the safer route.

"Give me five minutes to get comfortable and then we'll walk. There's a deck around back. Would you like something to drink?"

"No, I'm fine."

"Be right back."

Emma found cushy chairs and chaises on his deck, but she was too fidgety to sit. Instead, she stood at the railing, looking out at the ocean, wondering if her sister was still alive and if she was, *where* she was. She'd spent so many hours while Paige had been gone thinking about that—praying, hoping and trying to stay positive. But how could she when such dark visions invaded the others? Paige's car wasn't worth the bald tires it had been running on, so no one would have wanted to hijack her car. Had she had engine trouble again, left the vehicle and started walking? Had someone picked her up and then—

There were those dark thoughts that Emma didn't want to have, but knew she had to be realistic about.

When Linc emerged from the house he wore a blue polo shirt and denim cutoffs. His feet were bare.

"Ready?" he asked.

"Ready to find my sister," she agreed.

She kept her shoes on until they reached the bottom of the wooden steps where grass and sand began. Then she took them off and laid them on the step. Seagrass tickled her legs as they made their way across the sand to the packed beach.

As they walked along the shore, the wind tossing their hair, Linc asked, "Do you believe in things you can't see?"

Her gaze met his. "You mean religion?"

He blew out a breath. "No, that's not what I mean. I'm just going to lay this all out," he said. "If you want to walk back to my house, get in the car and go home, that's fine. But I felt this was an option you should consider."

"You're not talking about a private investigator, are you?" The spray from the ocean misted them as they left their footprints on the shoreline.

"Sort of."

"Linc, I can't afford one. I hired someone the first week after Paige disappeared. But he couldn't find anything and I couldn't afford to have him go on looking. When Barrett died, he didn't have life insurance. It was one of those things he kept putting off doing. Thank goodness I had my business, but with insurance costs and the mortgage, I don't have much left over each month."

Linc stopped and took her arm. Again his touch made her tummy somersault and her pulse race. But she had to focus on what they were discussing, not her reactions to him.

"Emma, this isn't about money. It's about a gift my best friend's wife has. Nathan's wife, Gillian, works with another friend of mine, Jake Donovan. Jake used to be a cop. Then he turned to private investigation. But after he met Gillian, his life changed. For the most part he and Gillian find missing persons, especially lost children. They started a foundation for this purpose. People they've helped have donated a lot of money. Funds just seem to stream in because it's a good cause."

"So Nathan's wife, Gillian, is a private investigator, too?"

"No, she's not. Nathan found Gillian through Jake as a last-ditch effort when his ex-wife disappeared with his daughters. Gillian found them for him. She has a gift. Some people would label her a psychic. She doesn't think of herself that way. She just seems to be able to tune in to missing persons. She gets sensations and feelings and in themselves they're not enough. But when family members are questioned, or Jake does research tracking down information Gillian gets, they've got a 99% success rate."

Emma was astonished by what Linc was telling her. He was a rational businessman and yet he obviously believed in what he called Gillian's gift.

"Let's walk some more," she said to Linc, pulling her arm from his clasp because she couldn't think straight with his hand on her skin.

Silent as they walked, he glanced at her every now and then. She could feel that glance, feel his concern and compassion for her.

Finally she said, "My dad left after Paige was born. We never heard from him again. My mom was really hurt by his abandonment. When she felt hurt, she went to church, taking us with her for the same comfort she found there until she died of breast cancer."

Linc stopped walking again. "I'm sorry."

She could see he wasn't just saying the words, he was sorry. And there was a deeper understanding in his expression that made her wonder about his background. "Thank you. The reason I'm telling you this is—before mom died, she took my hand and she made me promise that I would take care of Paige and if I ever had children that I would take them to church. She thought everyone needed to believe in something outside of themselves, just like she did and just like Paige and I did."

"Do you take Becky to church?"

"I do most weeks. She attends Sunday School while I go to the service. So what I'm trying to say is that I believe in something outside of myself." She looked toward the ocean and waved her hand. "I believe in the power behind this."

Facing him again, she requested, "So tell me more about Gillian."

"The way I understand it, when she was ten she was hit by lightning. It was after that the sensations started to come to her. She's a caring person. She loves her husband and son, and Nathan's daughters accept her as a second mom."

"And she teamed up with a former cop."

"Jake had heard about her, looked into her success rate and then recommended her to Nathan. After she found Nathan's daughters, Jake was a believer."

"Are you sure there's no fee, Linc? I can make a donation, but I don't know how much."

"They don't charge."

"But you've donated to this foundation," she guessed.

"I have. I believe in the work they do."

Emma stared at the sun beginning to set, the sky shot through with pink and orange. She thought about Paige and the empty car and dark nights when she couldn't sleep wondering where her sister was, crying because she was afraid Paige had been hurt, crying because she was afraid she was dead.

"Let's walk back," she said, needing to think about all of this.

Linc didn't initiate conversation as they walked, as gulls screeched, as waves pounded the shore. The tide was coming in, creating puddles in the sand that she was barely aware of as she sloshed through them. Linc stayed by her side, walked where she walked, a force to be reckoned with himself.

She would have kept walking, but Linc tapped her shoulder and pointed to his house across the expanse of loose sand and grass. When they reached the steps, she wiped the sand from her feet and slipped them into her shoes. He let her precede him.

Once they were standing on the deck, she made a decision. The ocean wasn't as loud up here but it still carried a resonant voice, a pounding that was a backdrop.

When she turned to face Linc, for a few moments the sound of the ocean faded away. The brush of the breeze on her face hardly registered because she got lost in his green eyes. But then she remembered why she was here, at his house on the beach.

Her voice was loud and clear above the sound of the surf. "I'd like to meet Gillian."

www.ingramcontent.com/pod-product-compliance
Lightning Source LLC
Chambersburg PA
CBHW030921120626
46554CB00001B/230